Also by John Updike

POEMS

The Carpentered Hen (1958) · *Telephone Poles* (1963) · *Midpoint* (1969) · *Tossing and Turning* (1977) · *Facing Nature* (1985) · *Collected Poems 1953–1993*

NOVELS

The Poorhouse Fair (1959) · *Rabbit, Run* (1960) · *The Centaur* (1963) · *Of the Farm* (1965) · *Couples* (1968) · *Rabbit Redux* (1971) · *A Month of Sundays* (1975) · *Marry Me* (1976) · *The Coup* (1978) · *Rabbit Is Rich* (1981) · *The Witches of Eastwick* (1984) · *Roger's Version* (1986) · *S.* (1988) · *Rabbit at Rest* (1990) · *Memories of the Ford Administration* (1992) · *Brazil* (1994) · *In the Beauty of the Lilies* (1996) · *Toward the End of Time* (1997)

SHORT STORIES

The Same Door (1959) · *Pigeon Feathers* (1962) · *Olinger Stories* (a selection, 1964) · *The Music School* (1966) · *Bech: A Book* (1970) · *Museums and Women* (1972) · *Problems* (1979) · *Too Far to Go* (a selection, 1979) · *Bech Is Back* (1982) · *Trust Me* (1987) · *The Afterlife* (1994) · *Bech at Bay* (1998)

ESSAYS AND CRITICISM

Assorted Prose (1965) · *Picked-Up Pieces* (1975) · *Hugging the Shore* (1983) · *Just Looking* (1989) · *Odd Jobs* (1991) · *Golf Dreams: Writings on Golf* (1996) · *More Matter* (1999)

PLAY

Buchanan Dying (1974)

MEMOIRS

Self-Consciousness (1989)

CHILDREN'S BOOKS

The Magic Flute (1962) · *The Ring* (1964) · *A Child's Calendar* (1965) · *Bottom's Dream* (1969) · *A Helpful Alphabet of Friendly Objects* (1996)

GERTRUDE
AND
CLAUDIUS

John Updike

GERTRUDE
AND
CLAUDIUS

Alfred A. Knopf   *New York*

2000

THIS IS A BORZOI BOOK
PUBLISHED BY ALFRED A. KNOPF

Phrases of Provençal poetry are taken from *Lyrics of the
Troubadours and Trouvères: An Anthology and a History*,
edited by Frederick Goldin (New York: Doubleday and
Co., 1973; reprinted Gloucester, Mass.: Peter Smith,
1983).

Library of Congress Cataloging-in-Publication Data

Updike, John.
   Gertrude and Claudius / John Updike.—1st ed.
      p.   cm.
   ISBN 0-375-40908-4
   I. Title.
PS3571.P4G47   2000
813'.54—dc21   99-33436
                                                    CIP

Manufactured in the United States of America
First Edition

To Martha

De dezir mos cors no fina
vas selha ren qu'ieu pus am

Foreword

THE NAMES in Part I are taken from the account of the ancient Hamlet legend in the *Historia Danica* of Saxo Grammaticus, a late-twelfth-century Latin text first printed in Paris in 1514. The spellings in Part II come from the fifth volume of François de Belleforest's *Histoires tragiques*, a free adaptation of Saxo printed in Paris in 1576 (Sir Israel Gollancz's *Sources of Hamlet* [1926] reprints the 1582 edition) and translated into English in 1608, probably as a result of Shakespeare's play's popularity. The name Corambis occurs in the First Quarto version (1603) and recurs as Corambus in the German *Der bestrafte Brudermord oder Prinz Hamlet aus Daennemark* (first printed in 1781 from a lost manuscript dated 1710), a much-shortened debasement of Shakespeare's play or of the lost so-called *Ur-Hamlet* from the 1580s, plausibly conjectured to be by Thomas Kyd and to have been acquired for reworking by the Chamberlain's Men, the theatrical company to which Shakespeare—whose names are used in Part III—belonged.

GERTRUDE
AND
CLAUDIUS

I

THE KING was irate. His daughter, Gerutha, though but a plump sixteen, had voiced reluctance to marry the nobleman of his choice, Horwendil the Jute, a beefy warrior in every way suitable, if Jutes could ever suit in marriage a Zealand maiden born and reared in the royal castle of Elsinore. "To disobey the King is treason," Rorik admonished his child, the roses in whose thin-skinned cheeks flared with defiance and distress. "When the culprit is the realm's only princess," he went on, "the crime becomes incestuous and self-injuring."

"In every way suitable to *you*," Gerutha said, pursuing her own instincts, shadows chased into the far corners of her mind by the regal glare her father cast. "But I found him unsubtle."

"Unsubtle! He has all the warrior wit a loyal Dane

needs! Horwendil slew the tormentor of our coasts, King Koll of Norway, by taking his long sword in two hands, thus baring his own chest; but, before he could be stabbed there, he shattered Koll's shield and cut off the Norseman's foot so the blood poured clean out of him! As he lay turning the sands beneath him into mud, Koll bargained the terms of his funeral, which his young slayer granted graciously."

"I suppose that could pass for nicety," said Gerutha, "in the dark old days, when the deeds of the sagas were being wrought, and men and gods and natural forces were all as one."

Rorik protested, "Horwendil is a thoroughly modern man—my battle-mate Gerwindil's worthy son. He has proven a most apt co-governor of Jutland, with his rather less prepossessing brother, Feng. An apt governor *solus*, I might say, since Feng is forever off in the south, fighting on behalf of the Holy Roman Emperor or whoever else trusts his arm and his agile tongue. Fighting and whoring, it is said. The people love him. Horwendil. They do not love Feng."

"The very qualities that make for public love," Gerutha responded, her rosy blush slowly subsiding as the moment of most heated opposition between father and daughter passed, "may impede love in private. In our fleeting contacts, Horwendil has treated me with an unfeeling, standard courtesy—as a court ornament whose real worth derives from my kinship with you. Or else he has looked through me entirely, with eyes that see only the rivalrous doings of other men. This is the gallant who, having laid Koll and sufficient gold on the buried black ship to the next life, pursued and butchered the slain man's sister, Sela, with no merciful allowance for the frailty of her sex."

"Sela was a warrior, a rover, to equal a man. She deserved a man's death."

The phrase piqued Gerutha. "Is a woman's death less than a man's, I wonder? I think death for both is exactly as big as it must be, like the moon when it blackens the sun, to eclipse life completely, even to the last breath, which perhaps will be a sigh over opportunities wasted and happiness missed. Sela was a rover, but no woman wants to be a mere piece of furniture, to be bartered for and then sat upon."

So defiant a formula, emerging from his fair daughter's flushed face, lifted Rorik's tangled half-gray eyebrows in synchrony with his upper lip, from which a long limp mustache drooped. His lip stopped lifting as his instinctive indulgent laugh was checked and hardened, by the pressure of royal policy, into a snarl. He was reminding himself to be stern. His mouth looked meaty and twisty and red between his mustache and his uncombed, grizzled beard. He would have been ugly, had he not been her father. "Since your mother's untimely death, my dear child, your happiness has been my supreme concern. But I have pledged you to Horwendil, and if a king's word is broken, the kingdom cracks. All the three years when Horwendil roved, seizing trophies from Koll's hoard and Sela's palace and a dozen or more fat ports of Sweathland and Rus, he allowed me as his liege-lord the pick of the plunder."

"And I am to be the plunder in exchange," Gerutha

observed. She was an ample, serene, dewy, and sensible girl. Had her beauty a flaw, it was a small gap between her front teeth, as if too broad a smile had once pulled the space forever open. Her hair, unbound as became a virgin, was the red of copper diluted by the tin of sunlight. A warmth surrounded her, an aura noticeable since infancy; her nurses in the icy straw-floored chambers of Elsinore had loved to clasp the resilient little body to their breasts. Bracelets of twisted bronze, brooches worked into a maze of interlaced ribbons, and a heavy necklace of thin-beaten silver scales bespoke a father's lavishing love. Her mother, Ona, had died on the farthest verge of memory, when the child was three and feverish with the same ague that carried off the frail mother while sparing the sturdy child. Ona had been dark, a Wendish captive. An unsmiling face with lowered lids and thick brows, a melody sung with an accent even a toddler could recognize as strange, and a touch of tender but chilly fingers formed the bulk of maternal treasure Gerutha held in her memory. She was pleased now to hear, in her father's mention of Sela, that women can be warriors. She felt warrior blood within her—warrior pride, warrior daring. There was a time, three or four years after her mother's death, when she thought that she and the children whom, in the absence of brothers and sisters, she played with—the children of courtiers and retainers, of ladies-in-waiting, even of the kitchen thralls, in the informal rustic arrangements of Elsinore—were of the same status. Then she became aware, long before puberty had awoken any urge to mate, of her father's blood regal within her. In the absence of a brother, she stood nearest the throne, this nearness to be assumed by the man whom she would marry. So some of the power of state was hers, in this mismatched struggle of wills.

Her father asked her, "What distinct fault have you found in Horwendil?"

"None—which is perhaps a fault in itself. I am told that a wife completes a man. Horwendil feels himself complete already."

"No unwived man feels so, though he may not proclaim it," said Rorik, himself unwived, in a grave voice.

Was this meant to soften her, so she could be bent more easily to his command? That she would eventually yield, both knew. He was a king, all substance, in essence immortal, and she of an evanescent loveliness, negligible amid the historical imperatives of dynasty and alliance. "Truly," Rorik pleaded, "is there no chance of Horwendil pleasing you? Have you already such strict notions of what a husband should be? Believe me, Gerutha, in the rough world of men, he is a more than fine specimen. He sees his duties and keeps his vows. Since your veins carry kingship in them, I have chosen for you a man fit to be king." He dropped his voice, with its cunning political range of threat and entreaty, into a register of irresistible gentleness. "My dear daughter: love is so natural a condition for men and women that, given normal health and an approximate parity of endowment, it will all but inevitably follow upon cohabitation and the many shared incidents of married life. You and Horwendil are fine specimens of our northern vigor—blond beasts, one could say, as solid as runestones in an upland pasture. Your sons will be giants, and conquerors of giants!

"You did not live long enough to know your mother," Rorik went on without a pause, as if all this were a single story in aid of his pleading, "but you in your glowing ripeness bear testimony to our love. You fought your way into being through your mother's reluctant, narrow channels. In truth, she and I were content enough with each other; we did not beg Heaven for a child. She was a Wendish princess, as you have more than once been told, brought back from the south by my father, the great Hother, in the wake of a murderous raid. What you have not been told, until this interview, is that she hated me, the son of her father's slayer, right up to the sacred ceremony and beyond. She was dark-haired and white-skinned and for six months with fingernails and teeth and all the strength of her slender limbs defeated my efforts to possess her. When I did at last possess her, taking advantage of her weakness after one of her illnesses, she attempted to end her life with a dagger, she so loathed herself for submitting to this pollution—the pollution at the root of life. Yet, within another six months, my persistent gentleness, and countless of the small courtesies and favors whereby a husband pays homage to a cherished wife, did work love within her. Her old enmity lived on as a special blaze in her passion, a rage that again and again fell short of being satisfied. Again and again we were driven together as if to find in our coupling—dark and fair, Wend and Dane—the resolution of the world's mystery.

"Now, if from a beginning so unpromising such an attachment could grow, how can your relation with the honorable, the admirable, the heroic Horwendil fail? He is virtually your cousin, by the bonds of alliance between his father and your own." Rorik's hand, an old man's hand, knobby and mottled and as light as if hollow, was lifted on the wave of his insistent murmurous eloquence and rested, like driftwood nudged forward by the froth, on his daughter's. "Repose in my decision, little Gerutha," urged the King. "Lend yourself without stint to this match. Some lives bear an enchantment, I do believe. Since your bloody birth, which weakened your poor mother ever after, you have displayed an extra quantity of that which gives others happiness. Call it sunlight, or sense, or a sweet simplicity. You cannot help but enamor your husband, as you since your infancy have enamored me."

It is hard, Gerutha thought, to consider one man when another is present. Horwendil—who was deemed quite handsome, with his candle-pale skin, his curly flaxen hair, his short straight nose, his icy blue eyes long as minnows in his wide face, his thin-lipped mouth with its strict look—stood in her mind rendered small by even the near future's distance from her. Whereas Rorik was here, his hand touching hers, his profoundly known visage a foot from her own, a translucent wart in the crease above one nostril of his large, porous hooked nose. A regal weariness emanated from all his creases, along with a leathery smell, his thick skin browned in the salt and sun of his youth's sea-raids across the rimy Baltic and up the great unpeopled rivers of Rus. His robes, not the velvet ermine-trimmed robes of a state occasion but the undyed wadmal he wore within the family apartments, had the secret little greasy stink of sheep in the rain. Her bones vibrated to the familiar rumble of his voice's rote endearments, and her skull felt the paternal pressure of his other hand cupped on her head in blessing. Gerutha found herself, as if cuffed from behind, kneeling before him in a spasm of filial feeling.

On his side, Rorik, leaning over to kiss the neat gash of the bone-white scalp where her hair was centrally parted, was conscious of a tingle on his face as of tiny snowflakes; stray individual hairs, too fine to be seen, had rebelled against the brushed order of his daughter's coiffure, held by a jewelled chaplet like a dainty version of his own cumbersome, eight-sided crown, which he donned on those same state occasions as warranted the confining, all but immobilizing robes of velvet and ermine. He pulled his face back from the sensation of her excessively vigorous hair and experienced a start of guilt, her pose before him was so demurely slavish—that of a captured slave, drugged with hellebore, about to be sacrificed.

But marriage to Horwendil, with a queendom all but certain with it, was no such slavery, surely. What did women want? There had been that in Ona which he had never reached, save in the instant when their bodies clasped and found release in a brainless rhythm of thrust and counterthrust, her pelvis as active in the business as his—a passion as if to be sacrificed, to be consumed in this act of, after all, capture. Then, in the next instant, their sweats still wet on the bedclothes and their breathing fluttering back into their chests like two homing doves, she would begin to recede. Or was it he receding, the capture achieved and he the lighter for it? They had been like a pair of conspiring cutthroats met in the dark and, their furtive transaction accomplished, swiftly and unceremoniously parted by a mutual hatred. No, not hatred, for a kindly afterwash would hold them side by side a while, beneath the embroidered canopy, behind the linen bed curtains doubled in thickness so their struggling shadows would not show through, within the tall stone room patrolled by cold drafts and churlish servants, as their sweated bodies dried, and he and she would engage in drowsy fumbling conversation, his eyelids still retaining visions of her naked beauty above him, below him, upside down beside him, her abundance of untamed raven hair between parted white thighs having tickled his lips. They would talk, many a time, of their growing daughter, the radiant fruit of one such clipping—the child's piecemeal assumption of mobility and speech, the dropping away of treasured mispronunciations and lisped coinages as she gathered to herself more correct language and adult manners.

Gerutha had remained the chief, tyrannically single topic of their delight because no brother or sister followed, as if a door had slammed shut in Ona's womb. Within three years Rorik's queen was dead, taking with her into silence her midnight cries of release from that captivity of concupiscence which Eve's curious sin has laid upon mankind, and into silence also the soft Wendish syllables whose unemphatic mispronunciation of guttural Danish delighted him as much as any missaying of their daughter's. Ona's fingertips had been chilly, he remembered, and yet even Gerutha's scalp, chalk-white in its parting, tasted of warmth. Whatever harsh or happy fate in this life befell her, she had been born of love.

Rorik was entertaining his daughter within a small timber-floored and wainscoted oriel room recently built to adjoin the King's bedroom, in this perpetually revised old castle of Elsinore. Lozenges of red afternoon sun lay on the broad planks of oiled fir, making good the designation of "solar" for these upper chambers devoted to private residence within a castle. The room's shallow fireplace sported a plastered hood, in the most modern and efficient fashion. The luxury of a brocaded arras softened the stone wall facing the three-arched, two-pillared window and its view of the gray-green Sund that separated Zealand from Skåne. Skåne, which the Sweathlanders coveted, was a Danish domain, with Halland and Blekinge to the east, and to the west Jutland and Fyn, and to the south the islands of Lolland, Falster, and Møn. To keep intact such a realm, scattered and jagged like the broken earthenware of a dish just fallen to the floor, took all a king's strength and cunning; accordingly, each new monarch ascended the throne through election by the provincial lords and, since the advent of Christianity, the great prelates. The inheritance rights of royal blood were diluted in Denmark by the ancient democracy of the (singular and plural) *thing*, the assemblies of freedmen that judged and governed the affairs of each locality and, above that, of the province. A king needed election by the four provincial *thing*, assembled at Viborg. These traditions enclosed the castle inhabitants as adamantly as the multiple walls themselves, the accreted keep, barbican, gatehouses, battlements, towers, barracks, kitchens, stairways, garderobes, and chapel.

The chapel had seemed to the child Gerutha a doomed lost place, reached only after traversing in her freezing slippered feet the length of the great hall and a gallery and several small sets of stairs at an angle—an unheated high-roofed room smelling of a spicy incense that scratched her nose, and of the clamminess of disuse, and of the unwashed bodies of the holy men who in their robes shuffled through the service, lifting the circular pale wafer toward the circular white-glazed window high above the altar (so that she thought of the Eucharist as eating sky) while Latin was being chanted unintelligibly. Being in the chapel frightened her, as if her young body were a sin, to be avenged some day, pierced from underneath even as she sipped the rasping wine, the caustic blood of Christ, from the jewel-beknobbed chalice. The chill, the Latin, the fusty smells made her feel *accused*; her natural warmth felt chastened.

Horwendil came from Jutland to pursue his suit. In acknowledgment of services rendered the throne, Rorik had bestowed upon him and his brother adjoining manors two hours' ride inland. That of Feng was the lesser, with but ninety thralls, though the brothers had shared risk and hardship equally along the coasts of Norway and Sweathland. Feng was younger by a mere eighteen months, shorter by an inch or two, and darker and slighter. He seldom came to Elsinore, and spent much time in German lands, soldiering and spying for the Emperor, though the spying was given the name of diplomacy. He had an easy way with languages and also had served the King of France, whose province of Normandy had once been a Danish domain, in the heroic days before King Gorm, when every Dane was an adventurer. Feng's free lance had even taken him even further south, across those Pyrenees on whose other side a dry, hot, and bare land was besieged by infidels who wielded curved swords from the backs of long-boned steeds that flew like birds.

Feng had not wed, though like Horwendil he was drawing near the age of thirty. Younger brothers, Gerutha thought, are like daughters in that no one takes them quite as seriously as they desire. Why had Feng failed to marry, when his dark-eyed, watchful demeanor bespoke longing? His eyes, it had seemed to her some years ago, when he and Horwendil had freshly come to Zealand to claim her father's gratitude, had dwelt upon her with more than the passing interest an adult bestows upon a lively child. But she found it difficult to think of one man while another was upon her, and Horwendil was upon her, looming in his burgundy cloak and his shirt of mail, the fine iron links glinting like ripples in moonlight. He had brought her a present, two pied linnets in a withy cage, one black with white dabs and the other, the female, duller, paler with dark dabs. Whenever the captive birds fell silent, he would give the cage a shake and in alarm the poor things would run through their song again, a warbled cascade that always ended in a sharp up-turn, like a human question.

"Some day soon, Gerutha, you too shall sing of mated happiness," he promised her.

"I am not sure it is of happiness they sing. They may be crying out at their imprisonment. Birds may have as many moods as we, and but one fixed tune to express them."

"And what *is* your mood, pretty one? I do not quite hear you warble of our betrothal, which has been declared by your father, blessed by mine from beyond the grave, and applauded by every living Dane who wishes to see our race enriched by the merger of valor and beauty, the latter protected by the might of the for-mer." He spoke these rehearsed phrases steadily but softly, testingly, a gleam of teasing in his long eye, whose iris was so pale as to seem more mineral than organic.

Gerutha said sharply, "I must suppose your figure of speech pertains to you and me. But I already enjoy, my lord, the protection of my father's might, and believe that what you flatter me by calling beauty, possessed later rather than sooner, might ripen to my benefit and to that of my eventual consort." She went on, taking courage from his presumption of having all the valor between them, "There is no fault I can lay on you, the model war-rior by all accounts—the slayer of poor Koll with all due pagan courtesies, and then the unfortunate female Sela. You are an accomplished raider, leading your rabble to the happy slaughter of scarcely armed fisherfolk and monks quite naked save for their prayers. I find, as I say, no fault in your brave person, but in your approach to me, from on high, through the old sympathy of our fathers, I feel something of the pat and coldly expedient. I am just yesterday a girl, sir, and put forward my girlish qualms blushingly."

He had to laugh at that, as Rorik had laughed at her impudence earlier—a confident laugh, already possessive, exposing short, neat, efficient teeth. His rough pleasure quickened her blood with a pulse anticipatory of her being, her qualms crushed, thoroughly his. Was this the self-abdicating delight her nurses and serving women had already experienced and absorbed?—the complacence of the submissive prey, the female pressed into the mattress and basted like a spitted chicken between the fires of the nursery and of the kitchen. Gerutha as a ripening girl had pricked her ears at the tone of rank and torpid luxury with which women mated high or low spoke of the absent, omnipresent man, the "he" whose bulk intervened between their bodies and the universe. These women had grown sodden in having their lower parts cherished.

"You protest too much," Horwendil told her, with a dismissive tolerance of her resistance that affected her like an embrace. She shivered in the arms of this large man's arrogance. He had an ardor for her that, even though cooled by calculation, was warm enough; his being was so much greater than hers that a fraction of his will overthrew all of hers. Bored with standing in the great hall, where she had received him, he slouched a

buttock onto a trestle table waiting for its supper linen.
"You are no girl," he told her. "Your frame is stately and
ready to serve nature. Nor am I fit to wait longer. My
next birthday will finish my third decade. It is time I
showed the world an heir, in proof of God's favor. Sweet
Gerutha, what displeases you about me? You are like this
cage, in which a full-feathered wifeliness beats to escape.
Without immodesty, I tell you my person has been admired, my brow considered noble. I am an honest man,
hard to those that defy me but tender with those that
profess fealty. Our alliance is desired on all sides, and nowhere more than in my heart." There was a glitter and
clatter of fine links as he put his wide hand, callous from
holding a sword hilt, upon his chest in demonstration—
the broad chest which, in the popular account, he had
daringly exposed to King Koll's point, an opportunity
the Norwegian's years had slowed his seizing of by a fatal
second. Horwendil was baring his chest again; she was
stirred with a kind of pity toward her suitor, so defense-
lessly persuaded of his own merits.

She said impulsively, as if indeed trying to break from
a cage, "Oh, if I could but feel that, and hear your heart
make its vows! But you seem to come to me conveniently, out of a general political will more than a personal desire." He had removed his helmet and his curls
were fair as poplar shavings, a dazzling tumble to his
mailed shoulders. She took a step toward him, and he
leaned forward as if to give up his perch on the table.
"You must forgive me," she told him. "I am awkward. I
lack instruction. My mother died when I was three. I was

raised by servants and those women my father had about him for other reasons than to nurture his lonely daughter. I felt a mother's absence cruelly. Perhaps it is unfeeling nature itself I protest against—if I do protest at all."

"How can we *not* protest?" Horwendil said to her, impulsive in turn. "Sent from the abode of angels to live on this earth among beasts and filth, and sentenced to death in a misery of foreknowing!" He had ceased slouching and stood close before her, a full head taller, his chest broader than her embroidery loom, his underjaw sparkling with pale bristles whose half-scraped state bespoke a hurried, apprehensive morning; he had mounted early to ride two hours to press his suit. A certain broad softness in him, this Nordic beau ideal, showed least becomingly in the double-chinned underside of his jaw, and Gerutha wondered whether she, when they were wed, might tease him into growing a beard, such as her father wore.

Of what he had said, she liked the sudden warmth, but something in the sense of it troubled her: his vehemence confessed an otherworldly scorn and disregard hidden until now behind a warrior's stoic front—a bitter drop in the juices of his youth. He was not even in this moment of confiding focused on her: he saw her as part of a brocade, a bride of silver threads, rather than as a statue, a stone angel or painted wooden Mary, with a weight akin to a man's.

Now, brought near to her in the course of his spontaneous disavowal of the world—of any world but the one he was determinedly making—Horwendil embraced

Gerutha, and yet did not stoop to a kiss, merely bringing his taut, decided lips close to her eyes while his hands, clasped at her back, locked her against him. She struggled a bit, writhing, but the jingle of her girdle bells recalled her to the absurdity of resistance, in the witness of those in attendance upon this interview—her handmaiden, Herda; Horwendil's squire, Svend; the castle guards posed motionless against the hall's stone walls, beneath the great oak rafters—ghosts of the forest from whose anciently painted and carved forms hung tattered, faded banners won in battle by Danish monarchs long since entombed within history. She felt caught in the stillness of a patterned weave, her thumping heart flattened among its threads. Only the little finches, the pied linnets, stirred, emitting in their hungry rotation, perch to cage floor to perch again, broken phrases or peeps of song. She rested her pounding head and flushed face on the cool iron mesh of Horwendil's chest, and a linnet loosed a long riband of melody cinched by a blissful tightening within Gerutha's ribs. There was no escape. This man, this fate, was hers. Like a tightly swaddled baby, she was secure.

Yet even now, at the fought-for moment of her surrender, her suitor thought of others. "They feed on the seeds of flax and hemp," Horwendil said, of the birds. "Linseeds. Any seeds coarser, they fall sick in protest." She tipped up her face to remind him who she was, and he quizzically brushed the knuckles of one hard hand against her cheek, where his mail had gouged in red the gridded impression of its links.

Horwendil the Jute was in the main gentle, as he had
promised, and rueful and preoccupied to a brutal degree
he did not—she said to herself, needing to think kindly
of him—realize. Their wedding took place in the white
depths of winter, when the affairs of war and harvest
slept, allowing the crown's guests to travel a week and
abide at Elsinore for two. The ceremony consumed a
lengthy day, from her dawn ablutions and a cleansing
mass administered by the Bishop of Roskilde to the uproarious feast at whose climax the guests were feeding, as
best Gerutha could tell through her bleared eyes, chairs
and stools to the great hall's two roaring blazes, in opposite round-arched fireplaces. Flames leaped like tormented men; smoke escaped the opposed flues to lay a
haze above their heads. She had been weighted down
with so many necklaces of hammered gold and precious
stones and such a stiff wealth of velvet and brocade that
the nape of her neck and the small of her back ached.
Enough dancing and wine had freed her body to an animal heedlessness. She was now seventeen; she moved
through the flicker of firelight and the touch of damp
hands, male and female in the chain dances, slither-
ing hands greasy from the feast, while the players of lute
and recorder and timbrel sought to press their fragile
tunes through the shuffle and heave of drunken Danes.
Gerutha, the music entering her bones, felt her hips
swing and heard the festive bells at her waist ring and
clink. Her coppery pale hair, in this last night before she
must don the wife's concealing coif in public, floated

through air lit by dozens of greasy rushes diagonally thrust from the walls like bundled spears spitting fire, as if laying seige to the celebrants. In the stately procession dances, the bride and groom led; the steps were taught to them in turn by a Frankish mime with bells in his cap. Dancing was a new and clumsy thing; the Church was reluctant to pronounce that it was not a sin. And yet song and celebration were what the angels did.

In giving his parting blessing, her father looked for the first time in her eyes feeble—his visage yellowed by the heroic intake of mead expected of a king, his frame bent under the great load of royal hospitality, his gaze rheumy or tearful in parting. Did he see *her*, his child now wed as he had demanded, or did he see fading from him the last living remembrance of Ona?

A sleigh trimmed with reindeer horns and holly branches swept them from Elsinore to Horwendil's estate, called Odinsheim. The snow dragged at the horses' posterns so that the two hours' ride took half again as much, while the icy night hung on its shattered pivot above them, in a crackle of stars. An oblong moon burned on high; its reflection rode along over the bare fields stippled with stubble, the tufted glazed swamps. Gerutha drifted in and out of flickering dreams, relishing the solidity of her husband's broad body beneath their overlapping robes of wolfskin. He talked for a time of the celebration, who was there and who not and what their presence meant in the net of noble fortunes and alliances that held Denmark precariously together. "Old Guildenstern was saying that King Fortinbras, replacing Koll in the lists of Norse ambition, has been raiding the coast of

Thy, where it is most barren and least defended. The Norwegian needs a chastening, lest he seek to take Vestervig and Spøttrap, with the fertile lands of the Limfjord, and set himself up as Jutland's true ruler."

There was a timbre in Horwendil's voice, relaxed and confidently paced, an easy public copiousness of speech, which he did not evince in his preoccupied, reedy-voiced conversations with her. With her, once his suit met no more resistance, he was measured, polite, and conventionally loving, or else actually curt, as he hurried through Elsinore's corridors on business. He had readily made himself much at home in the castle. "Your stalwart father appears no longer strong enough to lead an army, yet he remains too proud to delegate authority."

"He has now a son-in-law," Gerutha drowsily murmured, "whom he esteems." Horwendil's wine-soaked breath bit like acid into the expanse of the starry night, the snow, the reflected light of the gibbous moon. The higher it rose, the smaller and harder and more brilliant it became. It looked less like a lantern than like a stone flung up into the sun's rays from within a shadowed grove.

"Esteem is good, but it does not transfer authority. When Fortinbras knocks, esteem cannot bar the door."

He waited for a reply, but there was no reply. Gerutha was asleep, returned by the motion of the sleigh to the rocking of the nursery, wherein her mother's slim dark hand had melted on the cradle's edge into the wrinkled claw of her ancient nurse, Marlgar, and the little princess's dolls with their faces of stitches and char-

coal lines had the presence of real persons, and names—
Thora, Asgerda, Helga. In those childish fits of fancy and
domineering that enact a miniature tyranny, she would
send them on trips, marry them to heroes concocted of
painted sticks, toss them to the floor in dramatic deaths.
In her bridal dream she was with them again, in her little
vaulted solar under her nurse's eye, but they were bigger,
twitching in a dance, their bodies bumping against hers
with equal size, their faces giant, with bunched-cloth
noses and eyes of clay beads; hungry and lonely, they
wanted something from her, something they could not
open their stitched mouths to name, something they and
she knew she could provide, but not yet, she was begging, not yet, dear ones. . . .

The jogging motion ceased. The sleigh had halted
before the dark doorway of Horwendil's manor house.
Her husband beneath his wolfskin pushed heavily against
her, dismounting from the sleigh. His brother, Feng, had
not come to the wedding but had sent from a southern
land of clever craftsmen an ornately worked silver platter; its large reflective oval skidded in her mind and
sailed off as the horned sleigh stopped.

"Why didn't your brother come?" she asked from
within her dreaming confusion.

"He is jousting and conniving beyond the Elbe. Denmark is too small for him, when I am in it." Horwendil
had come around the sleigh—around the horses shivering in their clouds of steam—and stood waiting, a motionless ghost in the moonlight, for her to dismount into
his arms, so he could carry her into his house. She willed

herself to be light, but nevertheless he uttered a grunt smelling of stale wine. Close to her eyes his thin lips grimaced. His face in the moonlight looked bloodless.

His manor was not small, though unmoated, and the rooms seemed low and close after those of Elsinore. No fire was lit downstairs. Men moving unsteadily, freshly awoken, led them in with torches. They went down a devious corridor to a circular stone stair. Long triangles of shadow leaped and shuddered ahead of them as they climbed. They passed through a bare anteroom, where a lone guard slept. Horwendil cuffed him awake as they passed. A fire had been kept blazing in their bedchamber for hours, so the space was stiflingly hot. Readily Gerutha shed her heavy hooded cloak lined with miniver, her sleeveless surcoat of gold cloth diapered in a pattern of crosses and florets, her blue tunic with wide flowing sleeves and a band of jewelled embroidery at the throat, under that a white cotte with longer, tighter sleeves, and, lastly, the thin camise worn next to the skin, sweated with much dancing. A thick silent woman with trembling hands undid the laces and cord belt and wrist ties, leaving it to her, in Horwendil's company alone, to shed the camise. This she did, stepping from the cast-off cloth as from a cleansing pool.

By the snapping firelight her nakedness felt like a film of thin metal, an ultimate angelic costume. From throat to ankles her skin had never seen the sun. Gerutha was as white as an onion, as smooth as a root fresh-pulled from the earth. She was intact. This beautiful intactness, her life's treasure, she roused herself—betranced before the leaping fire, the tips of her falling hair reflecting its hearthbound fury—to bestow, as decreed by man and God, upon her husband. She was aroused. She turned to show Horwendil her pure front, vulnerable as his had been when he had bared it, for a famous dangerous moment, to the possibility of Koll's thrust.

He was asleep. Her husband, in a coarse-knit boxy nightcap, had collapsed from excessive festivity, and from the three-hours' bath in winter air followed by this sauna of a bedchamber. One long strong arm lay relaxed upon the blanket as if severed up to the shoulder, where a naked ball of muscle gleamed beneath an epaulette of golden fur. A strand of saliva from his slumped lips glittered like a tiny arrow.

My poor dear hero, she thought, *carrying that great soft frame through life with but his wits and a leather shield to keep it from being hacked to death.* Gerutha discovered in this moment a woman's secret: there is a pleasure in feeling love that answers, as with the heat of two opposing fireplaces, to that of being loved. The flow of a woman's love, once started, can be stanched but with great pain. A man's is a spurt in comparison. She hurried her naked, glimmering body to their bed, a single candle lit on the stand beside, and found her own cap, folded like a thick rough love note on the pillow, and fell asleep cupped in the shadow of Horwendil's sometimes thunderous slumber.

In the morning, awakening sheepish to one another, they repaired the omission of the bridal night, and the bloodied sheet was displayed solemnly to old Corambus,

Rorik's Lord Chamberlain, who on the deep snow had skied over from Elsinore with a trio of official witnesses: a priest, a doctor, and a royal scribe. Her virginity was a matter of state, for there was little doubt that Horwendil would be the next king, and her son the next after that, if God were kind. Denmark had become a province of her body.

Days healed the hurt of the deflowering, and the nights brought her a slowly learned delight, but Gerutha could not rid herself of the memory of that first snub, when, aroused by her own bared beauty, she had turned to receive a thrust that was not delivered. An ideal lover would have stayed awake for his prize, however weary and besotted. Horwendil was lusty enough since, with many exclamations of praise falling from his neat lips as they skimmed her flesh, and with enough explosive thrusting to fill a bucket, but, a sensitive princess, she felt something abstract in his passion: it was but an aspect of his general vigor. He would have been lusty with any woman, and of course had been with a number before her. Nor was his devotion of a quality that would keep him, if away from her long enough, from making use of a pretty Pomeranian captive or a Lapp serving maid.

Horwendil was a Christian. He reverenced Harald Bluetooth, the father of modern Denmark, whose conversion deprived the German emperor of his favorite excuse for invasion, the conquest of pagans. History had descended to the Danes on runic stones: Harald's at

Jelling read, "The Harald who made the Danes Christians." Gerutha was more touched by the runestone Harald's father had left at Jelling: "King Gorm erected this memorial to Tyra his wife, glory of Denmark." Glory of Denmark: Gorm had known how to value a woman, back before the Cross arrived to dull the Danish spirit. The Christian creed reinforced Horwendil's tendency to moroseness but would not countervail, once he was on a raid in a long ship, the old warrior ethic of plunder and self-careless ecstasy. Christ was on all lips but in their hearts the Danes still adored Tyr, god of sport and war and fertility. A noble wife could expect to be honored but not in realms beyond the small circle that domestic peace draws around women and children—unforgiving realms where men dealt with the necessities of blood and competition.

Since her submission to the will of her father, Gerutha had gained for herself a reputation for realism, for reasonableness. She was gracious toward her inferiors and saw quickly into the limits of a situation. A good woman lay in the bed others had made for her and walked in the shoes others had cobbled. The ductile temperament of her sex enabled her to do these things with grace and even zest. In much of her being she could not help revering the man who possessed her, who housed and protected her and—this the key to all right relations—*made use* of her. To be useful and busy gives each day a gloss of holy purpose. God's heavenly will reposes here in proper duty. Without such repose, the days will shriek. Boredom or war will come.

For Gerutha's body was soon busy creating another. The first thaw of spring saw her monthly blood-letting skipped, and then another, as the grass began to green on the sunny side of Odinsheim's walls. By the time that swallows, returned from their winter paradise which she would never see, were circling up from the pond carrying wands of straw and flecks of mud to their balcony-like nests beneath the eaves of the barn, she was certain, and released to their chances the two linnets Horwendil had brought her as his courtship gift. It was the male, the darker, with the more distinct pied markings, who seemed bewildered, fluttering about in the bedchamber, perching atop an armoire behind the curtains as if seeking some new limit to his freedom, and the duller, smaller female who darted out the open window and waited, singing her song on the bent branch of a fresh-leafed willow, for her mate to join her. "Hurry, hurry," Gerutha mockingly chastened him, "or she will find another!"

As the creature within her grew, displacing organs of which she had never before been conscious, and generating inconvenient surges of distemper and yearning, nausea and faintness, her father was failing. The yellow shrunken look she had noticed at her wedding had intensified until he seemed the size of a child, curled in bed around his devouring illness. Rorik of course disdained to complain, but in her sixth month, when her own discomforts had yielded to a dreamy sleepy state of blank contentment, he told her, with a smile that pulled his mustache awry, that he felt in the grip of the blood eagle.

He referred to the mode of execution in the saga days whereby a man's ribs were hacked from his backbone and his heart and lungs pulled out through the huge red wound, the screaming blood eagle. Some noble captives, it was said, begged for it, to show their courage.

Gerutha had never liked to hear of such things, the elaborate cruelties men invented for one another, though pain and death were deeply part of the nature God had created. Her father saw repulsion flit across her face and told her, in the gentle voice that he had always used to urge a lesson home irresistibly, "All can be borne, my child, because it must be. My death works in me, and your child in you. Both will out, as the gods demand." Amused at himself for slipping back into paganism, Rorik lay a dry hot hand on her softer, moister one and said, "The priests your good husband consults never tire of reminding us that we each bear a cross, in imitation of Christ. Or did Christ pick up a cross in imitation of us? In any case there is enough store of suffering for all to share, and if the priests say true I will soon see Ona, as young as when she died, and I will be young with her. If their stories are fables, I will not feel disappointment. I will be done with feeling."

"Horwendil listens to priests," she said loyally, "because, he says, they know the thoughts of the peasants."

"And have connections to Rome, and to all those lands where Rome has planted its Hell-preaching churches. Horwendil is right, my dear trusting daughter—this religion of slaves, and then of peasants and of merchants, has the future in it. The infidels are being routed in the

Holy Land and Spain, and here in the north, the last of Europe to succumb, the heathen altars are so many idle stones. The peasants no longer know what they mean, and cart the stones off to fence pigsties."

Gerutha had been baptized and raised in the Christian creed and usages, but without fervor, in her father's sometimes rowdy bachelor court. Rorik's own view of ultimate matters—where we come from, where we go— she had assumed to be weakly conventional, like her own. "Father, you sound scornful, but Horwendil seeks through the faith not only to be a better lord to his vassals but a better man to his peers. He is gentle to me, even when his mood does not permit him to desire me." His demands of her, she thought to herself, had been, as her condition more clearly declared itself, light, even as her need to be reassured of her beauty had grown. "He wants to be good," she concluded, with a plaintive simplicity that surprised her own ears, as if the child buried in her had piped up.

"I would rather hear you say that he *is* good," Rorik pronounced through his pain. "How far short does his wanting fall?"

"Not short," she said sharply. "Not short at all. Horwendil is splendid. He is in every way suitable, as you promised he would be." There was some malice in her reminding him of his self-serving assurances. As long as the dying live, the living do not spare them.

"In every way," he repeated at last, sighing as if feeling the vengeful intent of her thrust. "Between two people there is no 'every way.' Even Ona and I, there was a language barrier, a discord of unspoken expectations. Each match will have its unmatched parts. The sons of Gerwindil have the wildness of Jutland. It is a grim land, where shepherds in their loneliness go mad and curse God. For months the black-bellied clouds off the Skagerrak never lift. Horwendil seeks to be a good man, but Feng, his brother, neglects his adjacent estate and has mortgaged much of his Jutland inheritance to go adventuring to the south—as far, I hear, as a formerly Norman island called Sicily. This is reckless and ruinous behavior. Did I mislead you, my dear daughter, by pressing upon you marriage to a son of Gerwindil? I felt my fatal worm in me even then, and wanted to see you safe in another man's keep."

"And so I *am* safe," she said softly, understanding that this conversation was Rorik's apology, in case one were ever needed. But no harm had been done, it seemed to sensible Gerutha: her marriage was an excellent one.

Rorik died, and the prospects of election favored Horwendil. Gerutha, to spare herself the frequent journey, had moved with her retinue back to Elsinore to attend her dying father. After all the pomp of his burial in the misty, flinty churchyard where the bones of Elsinore's inhabitants moldered—lawyer mingling with tanner, courtier with hangman, maiden with madman—Horwendil moved to the royal castle to be with his wife, settling himself prematurely in the King's quarters during those weeks while the provincial *thing* convened at Viborg.

Some few voices there were raised for Feng, as the brother, though eighteen months younger, who was wilier in foreign ways and more apt to circumvent the schemes of the Germans, Polacks, and Sweathlanders without recourse to war; war was becoming, as undisturbed harvests and commerce increased creature comforts in castle and hovel alike, unfashionable. Some others spoke up loyally for this or that member of the noble *råd*—the Count of Holsten, prominently—whose kinship network offered more promise of holding the pieces of Denmark together, here on the northern edge of a roiling Europe. But in the end the final vote out of Viborg seemed certain to name Horwendil, the slayer of Koll and the spouse of Gerutha.

Only Corambus, Rorik's Lord Chamberlain, took Horwendil's preëmptory move into the king's place at all amiss. Though Gerutha thought of him as old, in truth Corambus was not much above a lusty forty, with a baby son and a younger wife, Magrit of Møn, so fair as to appear transparent and so delicate in her sensibility as to be in her utterances fey and, even, melodiously addled. She was not long to outlive her second childbed ten years hence, and (to extend this glance ahead in our tale) Corambus was never utterly to relax his resentment against Horwendil, whom the adviser in his own counsels thought to be an uncouth usurper. Though he scrupulously performed the routines of serving the new king, it was the Queen, Rorik's only child, the only surviving vessel of his presiding spirit, whom Corambus truly served and loved. He had loved her as had all those denizens of Elsinore brought daily into touch with the amiable, radiant princess, and even as Gerutha became a married woman his love did not turn away, but lingered, it may be, to the point of jealousy, though she thought of him as old, and his official manner had early turned prudent, fussy, and sententious.

Even before the messengers from Viborg brought the foreordained verdict—unanimous, the four provinces agreeing—Horwendil was soliciting support in the *råd* for a strike against Fortinbras. His rites of coronation were perfunctory, curtailed by the assembling of an army to expel the Norwegian invader from his beachheads in Jutland. While these military preparations were hurried to their fulfillment, Gerutha slowly ripened, her beautiful swollen belly veined with silvery stretch marks. And as it happened, by one of those auspicious conjunctions that mark the calendars of men's memories, golden-bearded Fortinbras was met, defeated, and killed, in the sandy dunes of Thy, upon the same day in which the Queen won through a blood-eagle agony to bear a male heir, whom they named Amleth. The infant, blue from his own part in her struggle, was born with a caul, the sign of a great man or a doomed one—soothsayers differed.

The name, which Horwendil proposed, honored his victory, in the west-Jutland dunes within sight of the wind-tossed Skagerrak, by referring to remembered verses in which bards sang of the Nine Maidens of the Island Mill, who in ages past ground Amleth's meal— *Amloða mólu*. What the phrase meant the bards themselves, having passed the phrase from generation to generation like a pebble gradually worn smooth, did not know; the meal was interpreted to be the sands of the shore, the mill the grinding world-machine that reduces all the children of the earth to dust. Gerutha had hoped to have the infant named Rorik, thus honoring her father and planting a seed of prospective rule in the child. Horwendil chose to honor himself, though obliquely. Thus her new-bloomed love for this fruit of her body took a spot of blight.

Amleth for his part found her milk sour—at least, he cried much of the night, digesting it, and even as his mouth fastened onto her stinging breast he wrinkled his nose in disgust. He was not large, else her day of labor might have stretched to kill her, and not ever entirely healthy. Always some small complaint nagged at the child—colic, a rash in his crotch, endless colds and croup, fevers followed by a long lying abed that, as he aged, she, healthy and upright most every day of her life, came to resent as self-indulgent. As the powers of language and imagination descended upon him, the boy dramatized himself, and quibbled over everything, with parent, priest, and tutor. Only the disreputable, possibly demented jester, Yorik, seemed to win his approval: young Amleth loved a joke, to the point of finding the entire world, as it was composed within Elsinore, a joke. Joking, it seemed to his mother, formed his shield for fending off solemn duty and heartfelt intimacy.

Her heart felt deflected. Something held back her love for this fragile, high-strung, quick-tongued child. She had become a mother too soon, perhaps; a stage in her life's journey had been skipped, without which she could not move from loving a parent to loving a child. Or perhaps the fault was in the child: as water will stand up in globules on a fresh-waxed table or on newly oiled leather, so her love, as she felt it, spilled down upon Amleth and remained on his surface, gleaming like beads of mercury, unabsorbed. He was of his father's blood— temperate, abstracted, a Jutish gloom coated over with the affected manners and luxurious skills of a nobleman. Not merely noble: he was a prince, as Gerutha had been a princess.

She wondered if her own motherlessness was discovered by the gaps of motherly feeling within her. She allowed nursemaids, tutors, riding masters, fencing instructors to intervene between herself and the growing boy. His games seemed designed to repel and exclude her—inscrutable, clattering games, with sticks and paddles, bows and arrows, dice and counters, noisy imitations of war in which he commanded, with his high-pitched voice and tense white face, the buffoon Yorik and some unwashed sons of the castle garrison's doxies. The quiet hoops and tops and dolls of Gerutha's girlhood had no place in this male world of projectile fantasy, of hits and thrusts and "getting even"—for a strict tally was kept in the midst of all the shouts and wrestling, she observed, as in the bloodier accountings of adult warfare, much as Horwendil boasted of how King Fortinbras, in being slain, had forfeited not only the invaded terrain in Jutland but certain coastal lands north of Halland on the coast of Sweathland, between the sea and the great lake of Vänern, lands held not for their worth, which was little, but as a gall to the opposing power, a canker of dishonor.

As she had been without siblings, so was Amleth. Her failure to be fecund again, she felt, was God's rebuke for her failings of maternal feeling, which she could not hide from Him. She was troubled enough to mention the matter to Herda, the serving-maid who had seen her succumb to Horwendil's suit, some seven years ago. In those years Herda had married Svend and borne him four children, before the King's squire had been killed in one of Horwendil's mop-up skirmishes with the Norwegians, whose throne had passed to the brother of Fortinbras, a foppish glutton with little fight in him. Horwendil delighted in striking against the outposts of this effete King's loose rule.

"Dear little Amleth," Gerutha tentatively began, "seems so isolated, such a brooding, quirkish five-year-old, that the King and I have long wondered whether a little brother or sister might turn him more sociable and humane."

"So one might," Herda tersely replied. She was wearing white as a sign of mourning for Svend. His death last year—in a raid wherein a supposedly defenseless little fishing port, rich from the herring trade, had treacherously hired itself a guard of Scottish swordsmen—had left her subdued. Gerutha sometimes scented in her maid bitterness against the throne. Kingship collects grudges and enemies as surely as a millpond accumulates silt.

"Humane, I say," Gerutha went on, "because more and more I hear Amleth voice, toward his inferiors—

the footmen and servers, and his playmates from the garrison's brood—a certain cruelty, disguised as foolery. He and that loathsome Yorik are forever goading the poor solemn Lord Chamberlain with their tricks and madcap pretenses."

"Having a brother or sister, my lady, doesn't soften the soul, in my experience. I was one of nine, and some were shy, and some bold, and others good, and others the other way. We rubbed against one another like stones in a bucket, but sandstone remained sandstone and quartz quartz. The young prince means no harm; he has a good heart, but too busy a mind."

"If only his father were to pay more attention . . . Amleth mocks me, even when he apes respect. Not yet six and he knows that women needn't be listened to."

"His Majesty keeps an eye out. He waits until the boy is ready to harden. Then he'll take him up."

"You and Svend . . ." She hesitated.

"We were happy, Your Highness, as things go for the less well born."

"Your children—I envy you. You have them, and they have one another. Did you and Svend pray for so many?"

"Not much prayer involved, as I recall. They just came in the course of nature. They weren't exactly wanted or unwanted. Sometimes, it could be, wanting them too much dampens the tinder, so to speak. The spark doesn't catch. And, the King being so much away expanding his realm and smiting the Norwegians the way he does, maybe he misses the time. It's God's will, and God's mystery. The trouble for most of us isn't how to make 'em, but how to feed 'em."

Gerutha stiffened, unwilling to see herself as her lessers saw her, as a queen ignorant of the common load. "How strange of God," she agreed, "to bestow children upon those who cannot feed them and to deny them to those that could many times over."

Herda paused, looking puffed up with perplexity, her pursed lips a stopper in a pink face. Then: "May I ask, have you much discussed your wanting another offspring with your lord the King?"

"As often as would be seemly. He is keener even than I to have more heirs. He envisions a succession, and does not like it hanging by a single thread. The Prince is not robust. His nervous temperament is susceptible to every shock."

"It may be a sibling at this stage would be a shock. The King has a brother, and I have not heard His Majesty take much comfort from the fact."

"Feng has chosen to abandon Denmark and pursue his fortunes in the progressive realms to the south."

"As a kindness to the King, it may be. Absence can be a present. Concerning the delicate matter of which Your Highness flattered me to speak, a midwife might offer more detailed advice, though she would be fearful in these high places of seeming to know too much and being in the end hung as a witch or drawn and quartered as a traitor. My own advice would be to let nature follow its course, where we have such little choice in the matter. There's a shape in things, fiddle and fuss however we will around the edges."

"I shall strive to be more humble and submissive," Gerutha sharply concluded, annoyed with herself for having sought wisdom in so lowly a place.

Years passed, and, though the Queen rarely shunned a wife's bed-duty, the Prince remained an only child. As he aged into the first stages of manhood, growing suddenly leggy and his upper lip displaying a silken proto-mustache, Gerutha, nagged ever more strongly by a sense of estrangement from all that should gratify her, turned to Corambus, the last living official of Rorik's court and a man whose affection for her she felt to be as old as she. If her father had been the life-giving sun, Corambus had been the reflective moon, moving at a harmonious distance, beaming down upon her when Rorik had been out of sight. His greeting, given several times a day as their paths crossed in Elsinore's stone labyrinth—"How fares my gracious lady?"—was met on this one occasion by a request, plaintive beneath its regal dignity, for a brief audience. She received him an hour later within the fir-floored oriel solar that had once been Rorik's chamber but which she had appropriated as her private closet, for romance-reading and embroidery and gazing from her two-pillared triple window toward the gray-green Sund, whose restless, moody expanse seemed possessed of a freedom she envied.

"Dear old friend, adviser to my father and now to my beloved husband," she began, "I am curious as to your impressions of Amleth's progress. His activities, ever more manly and martial, take him farther and farther from my weak woman's scope."

Corambus had been thin in Gerutha's first memories of him, but fleshiness had overtaken him young, and, his high post demanding much patient sitting and feasting, had quite mastered his figure by his mid-fifties. Yet there was still something adroit about him; he moved crisply within invisible and supportive constraints, his framing notion of himself as a perfect courtier, a stout prop to the throne. Gingerly he seated himself on a three-legged chair whose flat triangular bottom and narrow spired back ill accommodated his anatomy, and tipped his large head (its rotundity emphasized by the quaint smallness of his ears and nose and the stubby goatee jutting from his chin) to lend a portly attention. He spoke in the twinkling, rounded gestures—a gracefully upheld forefinger, a deftly dropped wink—of a man whose physical substance confidently seconded his sense of his station. "The Prince has a fine seat on a charger, and rarely misses the straw man's vital area with his lance. He draws the bowstring with a steady hand, but is a trifle quick to release. His chess is indifferent, lacking a degree of foresight; his duelling enthusiastic, if short on finesse; his Latin that of one who can only think in Danish. Otherwise there is little to complain of. He is *rex in ovo*, as should, *natura naturans*, be the very case."

Yet the old counsellor's eyes were watchful from within his impressive head, under its stiff green hat in the shape of a brimmed sugarloaf; he was waiting for Gerutha to declare herself. His hair hung beneath his cap in greasy yellow-gray strands that had darkened the shoulder of his high-collared houppelande, and—another untidy touch—he had one of those wet lower lips that appear slightly out of control, spraying softly on certain sibilants, drifting to one side or another when relaxed.

The Queen asked, "Does he seem—how can I say this?—hard-hearted? Disrespectful to his elders, and callous to his inferiors? Somehow *wanton* in his moods, which are so strangely quick to change? With me he can be one moment affectionate, as though he understands me better than any man ever has, and the next moment be just a boy, turning his back as if I am of no more account than a wet nurse to the weaned. I feel, dear friend, an utter failure as a mother."

Corambus tut-tutted and allowed himself a knowing smile, a rictus that tipped his head and sucked his shiny lower lip sideways. "You accuse yourself where no other would think to. Not a mother alone raises a prince; the entire state is responsible. Having endured the labor, you discharged the major duty—God often welcomes a young mother to Paradise at that point. By giving the infant suck for a year, you performed what many a noble lady, fastidious of her high bosom, delegates to an uncouth peasant girl. As Amleth learned to walk, to lisp, to string together sentences, to make sense of letters, to begin to grasp the tools and usages and necessities of the world, you were attentive beyond the accustomed royal behavior. Shamefully often, a child born to be God's agent on earth is worse neglected than the offspring of a trull and a passing highwayman. You have done lovingly by your boy. Let go, my good queen. Amleth at thirteen is formed for good or ill. The quirks that disturb you I would lay to his predilection for the actor's trade. He must try on many attitudes in rapid succession. To be sincere, then insincere, and then sincere in his insincerity—such shifts fascinate him. How marvellous, to his student mind, is this human capacity to be many things, to take many roles, to enlarge one's preening, paltry identity with many half-considered feints and deceptions. You have noticed, I am sure, his animation and awe when a troop of players travels to Elsinore—how avidly he studies their rehearsals, takes note of the fine points of their illusions, imitates while private in our lobbies and cloisters the rolling cadence of their recitations."

"Yes," the Queen interrupted eagerly, "I hear him in his solar, orating to himself!"

Corambus held to his chain of thought. "The Church has done ill, I sometimes believe, in letting up, in these lax times, its imprecations against this unholy travesty of theatrical performance, which, aping Creation, distracts men from last things and from first things as well. And how close, come to think upon it, the boy clung to the late Yorik, until that tireless jester, shaky from all his merry dissipations, joined the mass of mankind in the last, best joke on us all. Your son loved him, madame, and loves all clowns and triflers, as releasing him from heavy thoughts of rule and self-discipline. Your husband sets the boy, it may be, too stern an example. But I have no doubt, when clear duty is set before him, that Amleth, though turning it this way and that in his mind, will end in doing the needful."

"May it prove so," Gerutha said, not entirely persuaded, and obliged to defend her husband. "The King does not mean to be stern; he is beset with the threats of an unrestrained Norway, a seething Poland, a rebellious Holsten, not to speak of the peasants and the clergy, who constantly resent the cost of government."

"Greatness has the disadvantage," Corambus tactfully observed, "that all less great are enemies to it."

"In honesty, the King is easier with the boy than I. As they more and more approach the same stature and follow the same pursuits, Horwendil speaks ever more lovingly of Amleth. It is I who, in the helplessness of my sex, entertain anxieties."

Corambus sat erect for a moment, arranging upon his broad thighs the fall of his houppelande's huge scalloped sleeves, and then leaned a little closer than before, and spoke in a softer voice. "Just so. It is not Amleth whose health seems out of joint, given the dreaming flamboyance and outward awkwardness common to the commencement of manhood, but, may I say, his mother. As a girl, Gerutha, you were radiant and serene; you warmed every heart. As a woman, of now thirty—"

"A year more than thirty, as of October. Amleth's age reversed."

"—you are still radiant but, in some intimate reach, disconsolate. Yet no visible discolor tinges your status, the highest a woman may attain in Denmark."

"Too high and too large, if I lack spirit to fill it. My hopes when young had been set on siblings for Amleth, for a slew of siblings, to fill Elsinore with happy noise."

"Children are indeed a comfort. Their needs supplant ours, and our being feels justified in their care. We hide behind them, in a sense; our coming deaths are lost in the clutter of family matters. My Laertes, scarce older than your tricksome son, already thinks himself his father's protector, as well as that of his little toddling sister, left motherless, alas—"

Gerutha reached out to touch the widower's rounded hand as it returned to his chair's arm, having dabbed at his eye with a voluminous sleeve. "Magrit is happy in Heaven," she comforted him. "The world was a travail to her fine spirit." The world, she thought, and the succession of stillbirths the poor woman had suffered between the son and the daughter she had successfully borne. In Gerutha's sense of it this fine-spirited wife had been worn to a wraith by the demands of Corambus's goatish lust.

The counsellor recalled himself, with a rasp in his voice, to his queen's vague complaints. "The lack of children leaves a woman too idle," he pronounced, "especially if her husband rules a scattered island kingdom, with miles of coast bare to foreign assault."

"My husband"—Gerutha hesitated, but she had a sore grievance within, and sensed that what she said would gratify her sly listener—"is all that my father promised he would be, but"—she hesitated again, before giving way to her weaker side—"I did not choose him. Nor did he choose me but as part of a personal polity. He cherishes me, but as one of his public duties, at no risk to his many others, or to himself."

She was bringing the attentive courtier too close to treason; Corambus recoiled into stiffness. "Why desire risk?" He leaned forward again, his lower lip gleaming. "You read too many of these immoral Gaulish romances, which would make idle, sterile adoration the main business of life. If I may speak with the frankness of a father, you should read and embroider less, and exert your body in sport more. You should ride, you should hunt, as you did as a girl. You grow heavy, Your Majesty. Rorik's quick blood turns stagnant in you and tips your balance of humors toward melancholy."

She laughed, to wave him away with his effrontery, in which she heard a jealous fondness speak. "I never thought, my substantial old friend, to hear you admonish me for heaviness."

"It was a manner of speaking—a spiritual heaviness."

"Of course. Good Corambus, it has much lightened me to have you listen to my idle thoughts. Just to speak them revealed them as airy, and groundless."

Doffing his conical green hat, swirling his abundant sleeves, the Lord Chamberlain took his leave, satisfied that he had offered what bracing advice he could. If he had irritated her, she had irritated him by asking that he give serious ear to a woman's vagaries. Yet it pleased him to know that there was a crack in the King's arrangements, a stir of unease near the throne. He bowed his way out, leaving Gerutha to her days.

O the days, the days in their all but unnoticed beauty and variety—days of hurtling sun and shade like the dapples of an exhilarated beast, days of steady strong cold and a blood-red dusk, tawny autumn days smelling of hay and grapes, spring days tasting of salty wave-froth and of hearth-smoke blown down from the chimney pots, misty days of sifted sunshine and gentle fitful rain that glistened and purred on the windowsill like a silvery cat, days of luxurious tall clouds that brought thunder east from Jutland, days when the shoreline of Skåne lay vivid as a purple hem upon the Sund's rippling breadth, days of high ribbed skies like an angel's carcass, December days of howling sideways snow, March days of hail from the north like an angry knocking at the door, June days when greenness smothered every vista, days without qualities, days with a hole in the middle, days that never knew their own mind and ended in insomnia, days of travel, days of ceremony when she and Horwendil were fixed in place like figures beaten in brass or else overanimated like actors, dancing through sheets of candlelight and forests of food, wash days when amid laughter and lye she slaved with the red-handed wenches in thrall to Elsinore, sick days when she floated in a fever and received a parade of soft-spoken visitors one of whom might be faceless Death taking her to join Rorik and Marlgar and Ona, Ona who had died when younger than she, and then days of tender recovery, days when beech trees were in long red bud and the willows yellow, days when a serving-girl dropped a stillborn child, days when Horwendil was absent, days when she and he had made love the night before, days when she ate too much, days when she light-headedly fasted, days that began with the Sund glazed like a lake of mercury beneath a pearly dawn, days when wind whipped spray from wild waves like flares of white fire, menstrual days, saints' days—the days passed, and Gerutha felt them stealing away with her life, all the while that she moved through such activities and engagements as befitted a Scandinavian queen, helpmate to a handsome blond king who with the years grew ever more admirable and remote, as if enlarging as he receded from her.

"The Hammer," Feng told her. "I used to call him the Hammer. Dull, but he hit you square on the head."

And that was how Gerutha felt on the days after she and the King had made love—hammered into a somewhat blissful submission, nailed down, dispatched. Feng, Horwendil's brother, had returned from adventuring in the south, having placed his sword and lance and versatile tongue at the service, most recently, of the masters of Genoa in its long struggles with Pisa over the control of Corsica and Sardinia. "The Mediterranean," Feng explained to Gerutha, "is warm enough for a man to swim in pleasurably, if certain transparent bell-shaped creatures do not sting him to death. On the other shore lies Africa, where the Muslim infidels refine their tortures and abominations, and to the east lies an empire of curious Oriental Christians, who send armies to dispute the presence or absence of an 'i' in a Greek theological term, and who permit their priests to marry and wear beards. I would like, next, to visit there. Their nobles, rather than wield the cudgel and broadsword as in these backward northern lands, prefer the dagger and have greatly developed the art of poisoning, so I have been told. Many insidious Asiatic influences are brought back to Genoa by returning Crusaders and their captives, along with much wealth and ingenuity of thought. You would like the land south of the Alps, Gerutha. It is hilly and green, and each hilltop city vies with the others, making endless work for us roving warriors. There is a jewelled, fantastic aspect not seen in our foggy bogs, or boggy fogs. The villages perch most astoundingly on rocks; the slopes are terraced up to every crag; and the people, who are darker-skinned than we, have a soft and clever nature, sunny yet assiduous in the practice of manual crafts."

"I remember," she said, "an oval silver platter, with strange intense linear designs all along its broad brim, that you sent to our wedding, which you were unable to attend."

"I regretted my absence. I thought I would not be missed."

"You were, by me, though we had not met since I was a child, when you favored me with a glance now and then. I have often thought back to how you seemed. The brother of one's husband is a figure of interest, providing another version of him—him recast, as it were, by another throw of the dice."

"It has been my fate," said Feng, with some impatience, "to be seen always as a lesser version of my brother. Accordingly I have travelled to where the comparison could not be made. His wedding to King Rorik's daughter loomed, I supposed, as yet another opportunity to compare my fortune unfavorably with his."

This man spoke with a thrilling freedom, Gerutha thought, in a way challenging both to her and to himself. He enunciated easily, with intriguing variations in speed, the words tripping and then languishing on his lips, which were not thin and prim like Horwendil's or fat and slippery like the lower lip of Corambus but ruddy and shapely, the exact amount of necessary flesh, like a woman's lips, without being exactly feminine. His lips were not cut like Horwendil's or loosely poured like Corambus's but molded, as if by loving and careful fingers. His voice was deeper—a more lustrous instrument, expertly bowed—than her husband's, and his skin darker, from natural tinge or southern sojourn she didn't know. He was one or two inches shorter: nearer her own height. "Eighteen years ago, if memory serves," he said, "the Holy Roman Emperor's diplomacy had sent me to the Kingdom of Aragon, where the stalls behind the cathedrals offered items of an illicit trade with the Emirate of Granada, artifacts produced by the fanatically patient hands of the infidels. The design you noticed is a writing, running opposite to the direction of ours, stating, I believe, that there is no god but Allah, and a camel trader called Mahomet is his prophet."

His voice had become dry and rapid, with a certain drag of mockery slowing some sentences as if holding them up to the light of irony. His hair was black and cut short, with stiff gray strands bracing the erect coiffure. There was a patch above one temple where a shiny dent declared an old wound and the hair had grown in pure white, to give a pied look. His eyes were less blue and less long than Horwendil's; they were brown and slightly slant, with dramatically thick eyelashes, like an actor's eye-rings of kohl. His nose was hooked, with avid flared nostrils. He appeared, though younger, older than Horwendil, more seasoned. He had marinated in a saturnine essence. Gerutha liked the creases that the exposure and wear of his travels had wrought upon his leathery skin, and the way his face was worn to its lean tendons, with muscular ins and outs. He had the wiry vitality of one who had escaped constraints. She sensed that this man could casually lie and deceive those who loved him, but this did not repel her; it gave his interior in her mind's eye something of his exterior's agreeably creased, contoured texture. As Horwendil had aged, his appearance had become prey to the tendencies of fair, thin-skinned men. The tip of his small straight nose had turned pink, and his upper eyelids drooped, and the puffiness of his throat and jaw and cheeks were insufficiently concealed by the patchy, curly beard she had coaxed him, when still a wife with influence, into growing.

Feng was forty-seven. After the legendary slaying of Koll, Horwendil had expanded and consolidated his fortunes and secured the kingship, while Feng set out upon the forest paths and crumbling Roman highways of the world to the south. He had returned now to Denmark to reverse, if he could, the decay of his mortgaged Jutland estates—pillaged by his neighbors and his overseers, while his peasants had been ravaged by plague and crop failure—and to establish, with some months' residence in the manor that Rorik had granted him, a place in his

brother's royal court. His largely foreign guard of sol-
diers, their horses and pages, had all to be accommodated at Elsinore, for days at a time. Horwendil
grumbled. Feng turned out to be a formidable convivial-
ist; he drank without stint, though he showed drunkenness only in an extra deliberation of his movements. In
the late stages of a feast he preyed, it was said, upon the
serving-girls, but this disgusted Gerutha less than it
should have. Rorik had behaved similarly, once his Ona
was dead. Feng, too, it turned out, had once had a wife,
Lena of the Orkney Isles, married not long after his
brother's wedding. Her figure had been as slender as a
fairy queen's, Gerutha gathered, and her hair so fine that
a length hanging down her back could be coiled into a
circlet no bigger than a wedding ring. Feng carried such
a lock pinned to his undertunic over his heart, it was said:
Herda passed on this servants' gossip, seeing her lady's
interest. Lena had died, it was related, of nothing more
distinct than her own unearthly beauty and goodness,
before she could bear a child. So many good women dead
young: it seemed a characteristic of these fallen, plaguey
times. Gerutha could not but wonder if her own persistent vitality betrayed a lack of virtue, some unstated pact
with evil. She was now thirty-five, regarded by all save
herself as old.

In her company Feng was irreproachable, and seemed
indeed to shy from her touch, when she involuntarily
reached out to brush his sleeve or tap the back of his
hand in titillated gratitude for some especially vivid or
amusing anecdote, some bauble fetched from this or that

corner of a variegated, fabulous Europe. She was unused to a man she could talk to, and who was willing to listen to her. Horwendil and Amleth would walk away from her in the middle of a sentence, to exchange masculine facts and to make their private calculations.

"My brother seems to please you," Horwendil remarked in their lofty, drafty bedroom. His voice was neutral and reedy, a stoic nagging.

"He tells me of lands where I shall never go, since I lack a man's freedom. In Venice, he tells me, palaces are erected on tree trunks sunk into the sea; the streets are water, and men and women go back and forth on bridges like so many little staircases, and use boats as we use horses and carriages. In Castile, it rains only in the spring, when poppies turn the hillsides red. In France, each village has erected a church the size of a mountain, dedicated to the Virgin."

"Such tidbits you could gather from your romances. Which may be where Feng has himself gathered them. As a boy he gave my father and mother much grief with his incorrigible propensity for lying. My brother is one of those people, gifted in many regards, and of course charming, who believe that there exists a shortcut to the prizes of life, whereby patient labor and fidelity to obligation can be circumvented. Because he is my brother, by the blood-bonds God has forged I must love him and receive him, but you need not be as lavishly hospitable as you are. The Prince has observed your tête-à-têtes, and is disturbed."

As they spoke she was helping the King out of his

jousting armor, undoing the many little latches and catches and knotted thongs that held the burnished layers each in place. Chain mail was giving way, as swords grew sharper and arrows swifter, to plated armor; in the overlapping scales of his flexible brigandine Horwendil seemed a kind of merman, bulky and gleaming. As she helped remove the articulated segments, and then unknotted at his back the supporting articles of leather and quilted padding, the effect of gradually diminishing bulk left him appearing rather pitiable and shrunk, though he had put on paunch with the years.

Clad in her own nightgown of undyed wool, Gerutha fetched her husband's and, while his arms were struggling with its folds, launched her reply at his enwrapped, hidden head. "I am surprised," she jousted, "that the Prince has deigned to notice any behavior of mine. Ever since infancy he has been steadily fleeing me, so as to embrace you ever more closely. He is tormented by the half of him that belongs to his mother. When he next reports to you the perturbation of his offended sensibilities, you might suggest that he himself show his uncle more courtesy of attendance. Feng very possibly finds my feminine company trifling, but it is all that is offered him, since you and Amleth contrive always to be elsewhere within Elsinore, or else away together on some superfluous foray."

"It is important that the boy learn the ways of manhood and kingship," Horwendil informed her, with that aggravating grave calm he assumed when placing himself on a higher level of authority. The public self he had developed felt to her so wearisomely hollow. King-ship had gutted the private man even in a nightgown. "Within a year, Amleth will be leaving us to study in the Emperor's domains, where modern enlightenment, guided by the Church Fathers' divinely inspired pre-cepts, is attaining heights to overshadow the ancients."

"Denmark has its clever enough tutors. I don't see why we must banish our only child."

" 'Only' not by any desire of mine, Gerutha."

"Nor mine, my lord."

"I would have welcomed a brood, to ensure that our royal line flourish."

"I did not shy from my duties, though the first birth was ominously hard. I was willing to face torture again, to supply the throne."

"The womb is the appointed venue," he argued, "the male principle a mere tangency. Resentment of our early betrothal, it may be, curdled your fructifying juices. They lacked no supply of seed."

Gerutha's gray-green eyes flashed like poplar leaves before a storm. "Seed sown, it may be, in such coolness of spirit it failed to kindle the willing soil on which it fell."

His visage changed; he blanched, then flushed and stepped closer as if to embrace her, this furry wall of a man, suddenly breached. "Oh, Gerutha," Horwendil brought forth, "I was not cool. I am not cool toward you now, eighteen years after our wedding night."

"You fell asleep."

"To spare you a drunken lout I did—to bring you my better, morning self."

There was something archaic in his homage, something reminding her of Marlgar's old-fashioned accent
above her cradle, that made the Queen flinch into
repentance of her angry mood. "Forgive me, husband. I
cannot imagine a man serving me more worthily and
lovingly."

Yet she could imagine such, at moments when awake
beside his snoring mass, or when in mid-morning, as she
lifted her eyes from the parchment page of a *chanson de
geste* describing El Cid or Roland, Christian heroes in
armor that fitted their lean bodies like a serpent's skin,
her gaze greeted, through the two-pillared window of
her solar, the bile-colored Sund and the bleak beckoning
strip that was Skåne.

November, even late November, when the trees have
shed their faded leaves and the wild asters have been
stripped back to stalks by the morning frosts, brings
its unexpectedly warm days, and on one such Feng
invited Gerutha to visit his estate. The King being away,
she accepted. They rode in an entourage, the Queen
side-saddle since the people must not see her with her
skirts hiked. The horse she rode, a young chestnut stal-
lion, felt taut and skittery beneath her, the springs and
sinews of him tightened to beyond what the brain in his
great long skull could quite control. Gerutha felt herself
inside this skull, seeing in two directions at once, the two
views failing to meld. Sunlight gilded the gray twigs; the
shorn farmland through which their strung-out party
passed released to the warming air odors of cow-dung

and rotting fruit-fall, of parching hay and smoking peat. Dark dapples like schools of fish fanned out against the sky's glowing white, an incandescent sheet cut up and scattered as the horses carried their riders into a copse of birches and pines and out again onto a ridge where a forsaken crossroads shrine to the Virgin held a jumble of plaster fragments, some of them blue. The land on either side of the ridge lay in strips tinted according to the crops they had borne, each exiguous fief jealously tilled by its holder, the boundary corners marked with conical cairns.

All this she saw and sensed through one eye: out of the other Gerutha descried herself, in russet riding cloak and diapered green bliaut that exposed but the pointed tips of her ankle-high elkskin boots, gliding through this rare adventure, under the protection of her husband's brother, out into the land that for her had been mostly scenery viewed through the wide-silled windows of a castle that had been first her father's and then her husband's.

Her life as appraised through this inward eye had been a stone passageway with many windows but not one portal leading out. Horwendil and Amleth were the twin proprietary guards of this passageway and heavily barred death was its end. Death, the end of nature and the opening, the priests of the Crucified God claimed, to a far more glorious world. But how could any world be more glorious than this one? Its defining light, its countless objects and perspectives, its noises of life, of motion. The children of peasants lined the village roadsides to see the colorful royal party pass. Destined to succeed their parents in thrall to these strips of land owned by others, they were momentarily liberated to childish gawking and guile-less cheers. In the dappled sky a flock of starlings ha-rassed a hawk, dipping and scolding and diving upon him while the lone predator pathetically ducked and mewed.

Feng pulled his horse, a slender black Arabian exoti-cally caparisoned in a Genoese saddle and bridle, close beside her skittish mount. "My brother is good," he said, as if looming in the eye of hers turned inward. "A good man. Earlier, he was a good boy. Always testing his courage, going onto the heath alone for nights at a time, hardening his warrior spirit with little mutilations, quizzing my father about battle and how to be the in-trepid leader. I believe at times he bored the old man, ac-tually. Gerwindil was a godless brute who never did anything on less than three goblets of mead. His most heroic exploits were carried out in such an alcoholic frenzy he had to hire bards to describe to him what he had done. In theory he was a Christian, but in truth he had no idea what it was all about, or who the Jews had been, or what Eve's sin was. His idea of religion was a ring of big stones and ripping out the guts of a dozen prisoners of war. But he had bowed to the conversion craze and let the priests into Jutland; the castle teemed with priests, and my brother and I got the brunt of their instruction. Neither of us could quite believe what they said, but we believed enough to make us *triste*."

"Are you *triste*?" Gerutha asked, less in flirtation, she told herself, than out of curiosity—itself a form, per-haps, of flirtation. She was curious about Feng, why he kept fleeing Denmark.

"Not when a certain lady is in my eyes," he said.

"A certain lady?" Gerutha's blood quickened with jealousy: Feng had found a successor to the lovely Lena of the Orkney Isles. Horwendil would never be capable of such abstract devotion. What he could not directly hit, fuck, or outsmart had no existence for him.

"Who must go unnamed."

"Of course," she said. "That is part of the rules. But does she know, this certain lady, of your devotion?"

"Yes and no, I think. Also"—pointedly changing the subject—"my *tristesse* lifts when I am in a city I have never been in before. But I am running out of cities, unless I venture as far as Byzantium or risk disguised trespass in the Khanate of the Golden Horde."

They had passed into the terrain of Horwendil's estates, and she could see, at the end of a lane lined with leafless poplars, the manor house, Odinsheim, where she had been brought on her wedding night and not until mid-morning been made a woman. Several of their party now left them, to gather information for the King, on the harvest and his rightful portions. The rest proceeded on to Feng's manor house, Lokisheim, which Gerutha had seen from afar but never before from within.

The façade was as wide as Odinsheim's but lower by a story, and of exposed timber and nogging instead of more costly, rarer yellow brick. Within, servants could be heard scurrying like mice at the scent of the cat. But they had put off lighting the hearth fire too long; the cold logs sputtered and smoked. The house's interior bespoke a certain military order imposed upon the gaps of neglect. The walls and open cabinets displayed sou-

venirs of Feng's sallies across Europe: a curved sword
with a bejewelled hilt; a brass device of spheres within
spheres, the innermost globe pricked with the arcane
pattern of the stars; two tall halberts crossed above a
crudely carved coffer with rope handles and iron clasps
in the shape of leaping fish.

"A Burgundian gisarme, and a glaive of Bavarian
workmanship," Feng explained with nervous briskness,
having seen her eye taken by the halberts' intricate
curves, the lethal barbs. "The Germans of Bavaria have
learned the tricks of the Italian north. These curious
chairs are Venetian." He picked one up and snapped it
shut like a pair of shears, and then open again. "They
fold, the slats interleaving, a bit like the threads of a
loom. There is all sorts of cleverness abroad, and less and
less trusting to God. We Danes are a backward lot; the
cold keeps us fresh but stupid."

He set the open chair, shaped like an X, near the sluggishly burgeoning fire, and placed a cushion of green velvet on the conjured seat, for her. She settled herself, and
he pulled the other of the pair of Venetian chairs near
enough so he need not raise his voice above the clatter of
the servants bringing out the plates and bowls, the knives
and spoons, the loaded platters of their noontime repast.
"His goodness oppressed me," Feng went on, extending
the conversation on horseback. "It was like a pillow he
was pressing against my face. He was all answer, with no
question."

"I once called him unsubtle," Gerutha confided in
turn, "and greatly angered my father."

"Subtlety is not yet fashionable in Denmark," Feng said, "but in Europe it is the coming thing. For a thousand years we have all been God's peasants, delving and tilling in the sweat of our brow, under the lowest possible clouds. In Rome, whose busy little bishop claims to be the shepherd of even the dull sheep of barren Jutland, I saw a marble hand, marvellous in its fidelity to the actual, emerge from the earth, where men were stealing dressed stones for their hovels. In Paris, the learned monks have fallen in love with the thoughts of an ancient magus called Aristotle. One of these scholastics assured me that God and His Heavenly mysteries need no longer be taken on faith, they can all be proven as rigorously as the laws of a triangle."

Somehow nervous, he was talking too rapidly, and looking at her but glancingly. "I fear," Gerutha dared say, with deliberation, "that would leave our poor humanity off to one side. God should have sent not His Son but a theorem."

This near-blasphemy did draw Feng's eyes, widened, to her. They were deliciously darker than Horwendil's, the brown of crushed earth with grass in it, the residue of a creation, like Eve's, which came second. "Tell me, Gerutha, what do you believe? I think your father was no profounder a convert than mine. They lived and killed with the innocence of animals."

"They lived as their survival and pleasure dictated, amid each day's necessities. I believe," she answered, "what the men stationed above me tell me to believe. Outside their credo, society offers women no safety. And you, my brother, believe what?"

But he was not her brother. He was so swift to reply she blinked. "I believe men can be damned," he said. "I am less sure they can be saved. After we eat, gentle Gerutha, there is something I must show you—a beauty that puts our thoughts of good and evil at the mercy of the real."

The food was plain but the better tasting for that, the smoked meats salty and the autumnal fruits crisp. First the party, to warm it after the two-hour ride, was brought wooden bowls of pottage whose strongest flavors were those of cabbage and coney; it was kept simmering, day and night, in an iron kettle outweighing a man. Then came cold cuts of ham injected with brine, morsels of goose preserved in honey, salt herring and cod cut in strips for dainty handling, and those little dry spicy sausages for which the peasants have an obscene name. Asparagus cooked and then dried, with cardoons and plantains soaked in wine to make them palatable, re-called the summer's harvest of vegetables. For dessert and climax, a platter of dates and shelled almonds was passed—exotic delicacies in keeping with Feng's foreign tastes. The human company and strengthening fire dis-pelled the chill in the low hall, so the air became close beneath the blackened planks of the ceiling.

The Queen ate with the other women of the party at the lower end of the long table, lest their ears, though secure in snug coifs, be polluted by male humor given li-cense by mead and hopped beer. Feng appeared to be so engaged in the men's growingly uproarious discourse that he never sent a glance her way, yet he came to the end of the table for her while still crunching in his teeth his dessert of a yellow-streaked red apple. His teeth were irregular but seemed strong and all in place; he had not suffered the humbling pains and extractions that had left gaps in Horwendil's prim mouth, less eager to smile than ever.

Feng led Gerutha outside, across a courtyard whose frozen ruts gleamed with the noon's melting, to a long thatch-roofed building that, from the whistling, fluttering sounds within it, she knew to be a mews. As the couple crossed the courtyard, the rooks in the overhanging oaks cawed in a convocation of protest and alarm; their racket was so sharp it seemed to Gerutha her ears had been suddenly uncoifed.

The mews had a single door, just tall enough to admit a stooping man. Feng, though shorter than Horwendil, had to duck his head. Inside, the floor of sand and gravel crackled and shifted slightly beneath the Queen's hesitant feet. The interior darkness gave her halt. The smell of rotted meat and the pungent mutes of winged carnivores assaulted her nostrils.

"It takes a moment of adjustment, to see," Feng said at her side, softly, so as not to break the web of restrained noises about them—a rustle of armor-stiff feathers, a scratch of lethal talons on a perch, a touchy jingle of bells, and the voices of the birds themselves, a mutter of smothered weeping as removed as is earth from sky from the high-pitched shriek of a raptor aloft, climbing in slow circles to make its diving strike.

The half-darkness brightened. Details came forth: the cages woven of hardened withies, the dung-bleached perches, the extra jesses and leashes hanging along the wall, the ghostly-pale plumed hoods holding the birds transfixed in an artificial blindness. Falconry had always seemed to Gerutha a cruel sport—an abuse of the wild, the perversion of a piece of unfettered nature into an instrument of human amusement. She had felt distaste for it since the first time her father had showed her the mews at Elsinore, a building grand as a church, its flocks allowed, with the windows safely gridded, to fly back and forth in the high, sun-barred space.

In these cramped and dingy mews she felt Feng's poverty as he must feel it, compared with the King's. Now that her eyes could see, she counted a mere quartet of live inhabitants, amid the musty wrecks of empty cages. No wonder so much of the sport's cunning leather apparatus hung idle and unoiled from cobwebbed pegs. "My absences have maimed my retinue," Feng said. "A half-dozen birds and two falconers, an ancient and his lame grandson. How much do you know of the sport?"

"My father afforded me a few glimpses, and my husband fewer than that. I believe Horwendil takes little pleasure in the pastime, though the royal mews is maintained, to impress visitors with the pomp of the sport. For some men it is something of a religion, I believe. As with the true faith, women are not ordained as priests."

"And yet only the female can be properly called a falcon. The male, a tiercel, is a third smaller, with half the fire and natural fury. Here is a young brancher, netted a few days ago and now being hacked, as they call it. By brancher we mean between the state of an eyas, taken from the nest though unfledged, and that of a passager, a haggard fully fledged, netted in passage as it were. Forgive what may seem to you pedantry; but there is a science of sorts that insists on its own nomenclature."

"I have heard these terms," Gerutha said.

"We call this proud young beauty Bathsheba."

By the wan light of a single small window at the end of the mews opposite the low door, Gerutha sought to see. The bird was held like a rolled-up parchment in a knitted sock, her head protruding at one end and the yellow feet, already encumbered with trailing jesses, at the other. The little head was black-capped. There were markings down the sides of her white face like inky stains bled from her eyes. As her own eyes widened to see better, Gerutha gasped in horror: Bathsheba's lids were sewn shut, with stout, even stitches.

"The eyes," Feng said, hearing her sucked breath, for her face in its white wimple was turned from him. "They are what is called seeled. It is for her own protection; otherwise she will be frantic with the possibilities of freedom that she sees about her. Her talons have been trimmed, and her feet hobbled with bells, so the falconer can hear her slightest move. She is intricate and sensitive and excitable. For her to become a partner to men, she must be constrained, as a baby is swaddled, or as a king is held to his throne throughout a day's sacred ceremony. She has all outdoors in her heart, and we seek to pour her, as through a funnel, into a convenient container. She is fed, Gerutha—fed easier meat than any she would be bringing down in her untamed state. Blindness to her is a mercy, a lulling into safety. Have you never observed how, to catch a goose, the gooseboy throws a blanket over it, and it instantly goes still, in a kind of sleep?" His voice was lulling in her ear, grainy in pleasing abrasion.

"It is as men subdue women with their sweeping vows," she said. "Are her eyes ever unseeled?"

"As soon as the falconer deems her ready for the hood. He is accustoming her to the human voice, to our touch and smell, which overwhelm a falcon's fine senses. To soothe her, he sprinkles water upon her from his own mouth; he sings her the same song, over and over. He stays awake night after night, keeping her awake with him, until she at last will succumb and accept his glove as her natural resting place. These miraculous creatures are not like dogs and pigs; the realm they occupy nowhere touches ours, unless we patiently spin a link and pull them close to us."

"Poor Bathsheba, I wish she could understand all your beguiling explanations of her misery. Look, at the foot of the perch, she has lost some feathers! She will be as naked as when King David spied her from his palace roof."

She held out a small brown feather, tipped as if dipped in cream. He solemnly took it from her pink-palmed hand, and tucked it in his belt. "Here," he said, "come meet Jochebed, the Biblical mother of Miriam, mother of Moses. She is a gyrfalcon, from the regions of constant ice and snow. She moults from white to brown and back again in the course of the seasons; you find her now fresh in her winter feathers. Gyrfalcons," he went on, his amorous unease seeking shelter behind an instructor's brisk demeanor, "are larger than peregrines. Bathsheba is a peregrine. Jochebed has been trained to hunt cranes in the marshes, but I fear is as out of practice as her master. If a falcon is not held to her training, she reverts to an untamed state, and bates in her jesses, hurling herself into an upside-down fury; she rejects the perch and spurns to eat even such a steaming delicacy as a rabbit's liver."

While talking, he had pulled on a leather gauntlet that extended nearly to his elbow. Clucking softly, ruffling the back of Jochebed's white neck, Feng induced the hooded bird to step, with its knotted jesses, onto his wrist. Murmuring to her, he carried the bird outside, to where the mews with its solitary window backed upon a great down-trending meadow, its grasses quick with the whitening motions of the wind and the hurrying shadows of the fall clouds, which had thickened and grown scowling since this morning's ride beneath a dappled white sky. "Behold: the falconer himself," Feng said.

It was an old man, Thord by name, wrinkled and bent by time but broad through the chest, as if to support wings. He doffed his peaked felt hat in greeting his master, his queen, and the gyrfalcon, as if members all of one exalted crew. In a scythed stretch of near meadow he and his grandson, Ljot, were engaged, Feng explained, in keeping a third falcon, a black-and-russet sparrow hawk named Jezebel, primed for a hunt by setting her upon field mice they had caught and crippled, twisting and cracking one leg to slow them. For Gerutha's amusement they demonstrated: Ljot, a thin-limbed, limping child with white lashes and a milky stare, eased from a sack and released a trembling dun body that propelled itself furiously, hopping and zigzagging in its maimed state, for the cover of deep grass. Just as cover seemed attained, Thord released the bird, who in a dark gust sailed and dipped and in an instant quelled the hapless small creature, which her talons then let fall to the ground.

"Sparrow hawks do not stoop from a height," Feng explained to her. "They glide and snatch by stealth."

"And appear to be too sated to eat what they kill," she said, growing accustomed enough to Feng to dare a note of chastisement.

"She leaves it for her masters. She has been trained to eat nothing but what comes from a human hand. Now let us show you how Jochebed hunts cranes."

A lure had been made of two blue crane's wings tied together with a horsehide thong. The child brought this clumsy contraption from a shed beside the mews and carried it off a distance on the scythed stretch. Thord, making a rattling parental noise at the back of his throat, took the falcon on his gloved fist and with a swift twirl of his other hand knotted a thin leash into the rings at the ends of the jesses. Still with that hand he pulled off her hood by its scarlet tassel.

The hawk's eye! It was bigger than Gerutha could have imagined, blacker and more gleaming—a pearl of pure night. Or so she thought until the gyrfalcon twitched her head into an angle of sunlight and a many-rayed flower of gold and brown was revealed beneath the transparent cornea. Jochebed's glistening flat head was so finely feathered it seemed bald, and a pepper of fine markings patterned her snowy neck feathers. The hook-beaked head trembled and twitched as the eye took them in, scanning the assembled faces for prey. When the eye seemed to fasten on Gerutha's, the Queen felt her breath snatched. Thus death would not overlook even her, as in her girlhood she had once blithely imagined, the world seeming then one endless morning.

"Look away, my lady," the old falconer softly pleaded. "A strange human face is poison to them, until they are thoroughly manned."

Gerutha flinched, hurt by the admonition, for in truth she had been accustomed since infancy to be admired. She glanced sideways toward Feng, but he was intent on the business of falconry, his dark gaze as implacable as Jochebed's.

Limping, whistling, Ljot whirled the lure so it battered the air; it was touching to see him run, so raggedly and earnestly, his white face flashing as he kept looking back. He set the clumsily flapping device at the edge of the tall grass half a bowshot away, and crouched out of sight. A weak, moist, insistent whistling arose from where he crouched. Feng explained in Gerutha's ear that the whistle had been fashioned by slitting a dried crane's larynx. Thord released the falcon; it hurtled through the air trailing behind it a thin cord, the creance, attached to the leash. Thord, making that throaty rattling noise in his excitement, let the cord play out as the bird flew; Gerutha heard it hiss in the grass. Jochebed, feet flared, landed on the mockery of the blue-winged crane. Ljot popped from hiding holding out as reward a furry leg of fresh-killed rabbit. While the falcon fed, the boy gathered the jesses and pulled them tight. The falcon was reunited with old Thord, who stroked with a stiff feather her cruel fleshless feet, her hooked beak with bits of rabbit fur blood-stuck to it. Feng explained in Gerutha's ear how, bit by bit, the creance would be done away with, and the variety of game would be broadened to snipe and partridge. Live birds, their wings broken and their eyes seeled, would be staked in a meadow, for the falcon's education. Thus, patient step by step, would the natural killer be brought into partnership with men.

What a cruel and boylike business, Gerutha thought, *what a cumbersome charade,* at the same time admiring a certain honed passion in it, this expertise passed like a much-sharpened scythe down the generations. Men must play with death, to make it less terrible when it comes. Feng took off his gauntlet, on which he had fetched Jochebed outdoors, and invited Gerutha to thrust her hand into it. It felt dangerous to do so, inserting her hand where a woman's had not gone before. The glove was too ample, and quite warm inside—warm from Feng's skin. Under his direction she took Jochebed upon her wrist. The bird was lighter than she looked, all hollow bones and avid hunger: lighter than a kitten, or than a basket of colored thread on her arm. The incurved talons made a tiny ripping noise as they gripped and regripped the padded, tattered gauntlet. Jochebed's lethal feet tightened, while her skull maintained its restless motion; the gleaming black globular eye in its socket was seeking the perfect adjustment, the precise angle from which to appraise Gerutha's face.

Thord abruptly slipped the hood over the inquisitive head, and eased Jochebed from Gerutha's gauntlet to his own. "Don't mean to be short," he said, not looking her in the eye. "But a human gaze affrights them. We bring them right tenderly out of the dark." His relationship with these birds, she saw, took priority over the feasance he owed his queen.

Feng asked her, "How did the sensation suit you— murder on your wrist?"

The sun's beams were being occluded; the cloud fragments overhead had swollen and darkened, piling up like ice cakes on the windward side of the Skaw. The short November day was quickly shedding its unseasonable warmth.

"We are females, she and I," Gerutha responded. "We must take what we can of what the world offers. No doubt she would eat greens, if nature had not made her a slave to flesh. We should not judge her by the rules we make for sheep."

Feng laughed, his teeth uneven but thrilling in that red mouth, there between his trimmed mustache and pointed, Italianate beard. "I would like to leave you a present of a pet. Not Jochebed, she is too much your sister, but perhaps dainty Bathsheba, when her eyes are unseeled."

"Leave me?"

"Yes. I must be off again. Denmark is not yet a nesting-ground for me. My Genovese masters consented to my absence on the plea of personal affairs; those affairs have been surveyed and their shifts reinforced. None but my falcons will miss me; my brother has Denmark in hand. Denmark and the lady through whom, in the feelings of the people, the throne descends. The country loves you, Gerutha, to even the most errant Dane." He curtly bowed, in case she missed the identification of himself.

It was one of the few unsubtle things he had done; a woman of course knows what is happening, what negotiations between the speechless lower parts are advanced under cover of elevated manners. "Errant," she said, "I hope not in loyalty. My husband the King has come to rely upon your attendance in his court. He values your present counsel and the accord of your shared past. You recall him to his youthful self. The sons of Gerwindil should not be so much parted."

"Perhaps they thrive best apart. Cubs cannot share the same den for life. There is a safety in distance, and a purity that leaves the loyalty untested, for brothers and lovers both."

"Who speaks of lovers?" Gerutha asked. "I will miss a friend and brother newly acquired—a brother-friend and falcon-lover."

"We belong to those who handle us," Feng said and, snapping his head aside as if in irritation, signalled to Thord that they must depart. Thord undid Jochebed's leash and creance and reattached to the gyrfalcon's jesses the bells whereby no motion of hers throughout the day and night would go unnoticed, and her handler could be always beckoned. The old man's eyes, it seemed to Gerutha, had been buried gleaming in the creases of his weathered face, over the years erased in deference to the haughty, oversized stare of hawks. Her heart went out to the boy, Ljot, consigned to grow old and bent, wrinkled and brown, in service to a race of ungrateful raptors.

Lord Christ, Feng thought, *this love of her is eating me alive.* Craving for Gerutha gnawed on him in the night, glimpses of her burned into the back of his brain as he shifted and twisted on his vagabond's pallet—a certain way she turned, a certain way her face would be tilted when she turned, turned at the voice of some other and not aware he was watching (or was she?). Her loose and gauzy hair, self-haloed by its own stray strands, would slightly lift, a wife's fair reddish hair it was an indecency to see, but that he was the brother of her husband and thus allowed to enter their apartments as they broke their night's fast, she in an unbelted gown not so long it hid the bareness of her feet, a pink bareness implying an entire body flushed still with the languid heat of sleep just shaken off, pink on the sides and white in the toes and at her bare heels thickened to a tallowy tint, Gerutha's whole body a flexible candle carrying the pale unconstrainable flame of her hair.

Horwendil would be there, already dressed to go hunting with that foppish rude brat Amleth or else in velvet garb of state for the entertaining of some ambassador or dithering clerk of the exchequer, quite ignoring

the female treasure demurely silent at his elbow, her lips
daintily embracing from off the sharp point of her knife
bits of sautéed wild boar or of a trencher soaked with
poached quail's eggs, her husband babbling pompously
away to impress his brother about the Norwegians or the
Polacks or the Novgorodians nibbling away at some
wretched marshy border or treacherous sea-route, his
voice bloated with kingship. Unused to contradiction, it
would hollowly roll on: "And the merchants, the merchants, Feng, are such tiresome rascals, they flourish on
the security the state creates, they use our roads, our har-
bors, our safe cities, and must be taxed, but they hide
their wealth shamelessly, tucking it here and there where
no accountant can find it! In the days of our father, Feng,
wealth could not hide, it was out in the open, crops and
lands, the cottages of the vassals and the villeins, grazed
pastures and stocked barns, the king's agent could tot it
up at a glance, but now wealth creeps, it oozes from place
to place invisibly, in the form of numbers, numbers writ-
ten in ledgers, it is easy to blame the Jews but, mark me,
others than the Jews are willing in this rotten day and age
to handle the dirty business of usury, to laugh at damnation, to strike the phantom balance of debit and credit
and make it stick from town to town, port to port, so the
cords of loyalty that in our father's day bound thrall to
lord, lord to king, and king to God were of *no* account, so
to speak, even the languages whereby hill-dwellers and
valley-dwellers once knew one another apart now dis-
solved in the language of figures—figures, my dear
Feng, invented by the Evil One himself in the guise of

Muhammadans and brought back by the Crusaders with many a fatal case of pox caught from some olive-skinned whore. A merchant's wealth, damn it to Jesus, is slippery as a snake: it shows itself nowhere but in the furnishings of his bedroom and the amount of silver and gold he hangs upon his fat strumpet of a hausfrau!"

There was, always had been, in Horwendil's discourse a rambling licentiousness, a furtive braggadocio as his tongue could not forbear touching his mind's underparts, the women he had spread open as part of a raider's privilege, even Sela, whom Feng had ineffectually begged be spared, exiled to an island or ransomed back to the Norwegians, but whom Horwendil had to have, though she scratched and fought like a Valkyrie. Thus stained and self-disgraced by many an easy triumph over a fair and helpless creature, the King obliviously droned on, the grease of his breakfast meats gleaming on his beard, his belly as swollen as that of any merchant he schemed to rob. That such a bulky human pig could with the blessing of the Church pollute Gerutha whenever his lust bid maddened Feng to the point of murder. She formed for him in her graceful affirmative bearing a luminous window into a purer world. When he looked at her his soul winced as light poured in. She would move from the shared breakfast table to her personal table by the window, with its oval metal mirror, and brush out her hair, her back arched in the supple morning gown, her pointed pink elbow slipped from its wide sleeve in the uplifted rhythmic motion, her pale coppery hair crackling and spraying in a thousand fiery ends. Feng's mouth would go dry in such near presence of her untouchable flesh.

That her body had an underside of concupiscence she herself had admitted in playful conversation with him. Lightly she spoke, in the conceits of courtly love, of lower parts, which the upper merely served. This touched his sensitive quick, and had been intended to. But he knew that she, with that skill of women which conceals from them their own purposes in too much distinctness, meant mostly to agitate a communion of spirits from within the impregnable castle of her position as royal wife and mother. She was thirty-five, at her peak of ripeness. As long as she could bear the King another heir, it would be extreme treason and an affront to Heaven were any other Dane to lie with her. The royal blood was sacred, God's blood on earth. And Feng's devotion included a self-protective austerity, an abstractness. He did not picture her underparts, nor the licentious poses that open a woman, like a mare in the stud yard, to penetration. The amused play of her mouth and eyes, the casual music of her considerate voice, a glimpse of her bare feet and rosy morning languor were to him amorous nutrition enough: at this delicate stage the image of more would have revolted him. Like a falcon, love was kept best at hunger pitch. What we love, he understood from the poetry of Provence, where his restless freelancing had more than once taken him, is less the gift bestowed, the moon-mottled nakedness and wet-socketed submission, than the Heavenly graciousness of bestowal—the last gown lifted and the dark frank frontal stare in the bedchamber challenging you to appraise highly enough this gift torn from Eden's shadows.

Gerutha he could hardly appraise higher. He loved

her good sense, her forgiving gaiety. Passed young from father to husband, oppressed by a husband whose virtues would appeal to a father, she knew her life had skipped something in its stages, but she did not nurse the grudge. So kind she was, so clear-sighted and natural. "Nature" was one of her words, which she used as women of other languages spoke of *der Gott, le bon Dieu, Iddio, Dios*. Feng loved the way that, even as her level gray-green eyes assigned everything its fair weight, her generous lips and the tiny muscles around her lips played together, as if words all had a joke in them which she could not help tasting. When she pronounced his name, she let the "ng" linger in the air, so as almost to create a second syllable. Her own name too, the rare times he heard it issue from her lips — for our names are used for convenience by others but figure marginally in our own minds, which know ourselves as an entity too vast and vague to name — was softened to "Geruthe."

Every inflection of her speech, thought, and movement seemed to him breathtakingly perfect. Even the upright little gap between her teeth was a perfection, a sweet surprise when she smiled. *Sas belas dens*, he remembered from a poem by Bertran de Born. *Vuolh sas belas dens en dos.* I want her beautiful teeth as a gift. A woman to be exalted by love must have a flaw, a weakness, and Gerutha's, as he saw it, was her malleability, a passive lax streak that had allowed her father and then her husband to have their way. Her affection for nature had bred in her a fatalism, a propensity to surrender. She would surrender to him, too, if pressed. He felt that. And she should be his because only he *saw* her. His brother had gone blind in his kingship and had always been thick, a dealer in broad, approximate, merely useful truths.

For Feng to live with Gerutha beside him would be to bathe daily in the radiance from which now he must keep averting his eyes, though her afterimage burned at the back of his brain. She would turn the lead in him to gold, lift from his heart the dark Jutish stain it had taken early. And—hardly to be considered, but a fact—she would make him a king. Denmark and Gerutha would be his together. So grand a possibility hovered a few feet away, as he stood cravenly attending in the shuffle of his brother's court. Feng's desire, when it took him from behind, was so strong his knees would threaten to buckle and his head would pound with impatience.

As the craving within him raged, his brother passed from contemptible to pitiable, hateful to helpless. Horwendil knew nothing of how his immeasurable treasure burdened him with risk. He had no idea, or at most a passing, frivolous idea, of his brother's lovesick envy. Feng must remove his dangerous envy from the realm of this wooden-headed monarch—defenseless in his pomp, unsuspecting in his fraternity. The ghost of their father, Gerwindil, watched. A shred of conscience tied the wicked brother's hands. Feng went south to serve again the Emperor's theoretical liegemen the consuls of Genoa, and farther south still in that service, and then east as emissary to Genoa's ally, the porphyry-and-ivory throne of Byzantium.

By way of farewell he had bid Thord carry Bathsheba,

her eyes unseeled, to the Queen at Elsinore. During a dozen years of adventure, of further hardening, Feng now and then wondered how his gift had fared. Pinned inside his undertunic of coarsest and most durable linen, he carried everywhere the soft brown breast feather she had handed him, as pledge and irritant.

II

THE KING was irate. "But what can the boy still be studying at Wittenberg?" Horvendile asked. "He is twenty-nine! I am all of sixty, with aches and pains and spells of irresistible lethargy. It is high time Hamblet came home and studied kingship."

Geruthe kept brushing out her thick hair, which in the half-light of this gloomy winter morning emanated a coruscating halo of static phosphorescence as she brushed. Some sparks were blue, and others yellow and remarkably long as they leaped from where with her brush of stiffest boar bristle she sharply pulled taut an extended coppery strand. The more she brushed, the more filaments stood up all over her head. "I think he finds us unsubtle," she said. "We drink too much. We eat crudely, with hunting knives. We are barbarians, compared with his professors down there."

"Unsubtle! What does he think life is—a theatrical performance to be minced through by boys in women's clothes?"

"He doesn't talk to me about what he thinks," she said, "or indeed about anything. But I understand from what Corambis has let drop of what Laertes tells *him*, there's a ferment going on in cultivated circles to the south, various bits of ancient knowledge the Crusaders brought back, the Arabs and the Byzantine monks have been transcribing them for centuries but nobody read them, something about a new way of looking at the world *scientifically*, whatever that is, letting nature tell us about itself in little details, one after another, as if women and children and millers and farmers haven't been doing that all along. Instead of taking everything on faith from the priests and the Bible, I mean. Instead of arguing from first principles, you deduce your principles from a host of observed particulars. I'm sorry, I'm not making a great deal of sense; it's still too early in the morning, my dearest."

"You confirm my worst suspicions. My son is down there on the Elbe learning how to *doubt*—learning mockery and blasphemy when I'm trying to instill piety and order into a scheming, rebellious conglomeration of Danes."

"What else did Corambis say?" Geruthe mused, as colorful electricity played about her head. "Something about man being the measure of things, which makes a kind of sense, really, since men and women are right here all around us while God, though we can all feel He's here *somewhere*, is a lot harder to observe. Still, you can't help wondering if people are ready to be the measure of things. We can hardly measure ourselves. We are the only animal that makes mis*takes*."

"We must get Hamblet back, or the regional *thing* will choose another when I—if I were to— As I say, I have these uncanny spells of fatigue."

"Normal aging, merely, darling. I too need a nap more than formerly. You'll live another twenty years at least," his wife told the King, whipping an especially impressive blue spark from her long hair, as if the thought were not entirely soothing to her. "You Jutes are tough as nails. Look at your brother. Five wounds in a Turkish ambush, and still he moves like a panther, with a bear's thick head of hair." It soothed her to mention Fengon, lately returned from his lifetime of knightly exile, and suddenly very attentive to those who lived in Elsinore. His scalp and beard, becomingly sprinkled with gray, flourished, whereas Horvendile's curly pale locks, once so spectacularly Nordic, had thinned touchingly above his brow and at the back of his skull. His skull showed its mineral hardness, its marmoreal gloss.

"Yes," he said loudly, stalking about and summing up: "My rogue of a brother returned and hanging as close about the castle as if he smells his future here, and Hamblet, who should be in residence cutting a successor's stalwart figure, impressive and engaging yet not too much so, off instead in Wittenberg wasting his days in fruitless logic-chopping and his nights in whorish follies that might not disgrace a nineteen-year-old but sit sluggishly on a man ten years older."

He was in his storming mode, like a sheet of tin shaken

behind the stage to signify thunder. Geruthe touched the back of her teeth with the tip of her tongue, not wishing to speak too hastily to this husband of such ponderous and firm impulses. She was conscious, more and more, of guarding and directing her exchanges with him, once so spontaneously confiding, even though he often gave her back but a grunt. "I do not think," she said, "that our son has much taste for those crass pleasures you rather enviously indict him for. As he grew, his induction into the mysteries of nature seemed to be, as far as a mother could observe, attended more by wonderment and disgust than by delight. He does not delight in females as such; he has enough of the passive principle in himself so as not to be uncritically attracted to it in others. Only through a very young and delicate vessel might Hamblet's fastidiousness be overcome. I have in mind—as I have mentioned, my lord—Ophelia. She is seventeen, the very age at which I was wed, and during his infrequent visits to Elsinore the Prince has paid increasing notice as her bloom has become conspicuous. This summer past, I believe, their relation advanced beyond that of a chaffing older cousin to his painfully shy and undeveloped adorer. She has become a beauty, with a sweet and impish wit, though still shy, as a maiden should be."

Horvendile said, marching about their bedchamber as if in blind pursuit of a way out, "She is not merely shy; she is fey. Her brain holds a crack any ill circumstance might jar agape. Further, a prince should wed a princess and thus enlarge the throne's connections and influence. To marry the daughter of one's Lord Chamberlain is unhealthy political incest. Corambis has so long flattered our ears with his counsels I have been considering his dismissal—to be phrased, of course, as his well-earned and well-rewarded retirement, perhaps to the little lodge by Gurre Sø, to whose enlargement and reroofing he has devoted so many trickles from the royal purse."

This was unpleasant news to Geruthe, who saw Corambis as her ally, in an Elsinore that felt colder than formerly. She hid her surprise, protesting only, "Corambis advised not just you but my father, Rodericke. He is a living link to my girlhood, and the simple hearty days when the Norwegians were freshly humbled."

"Exactly. He has grown too accustomed to basking in the King's power. Long proximity to the throne breeds envy and presumption. His scheme of making his frail daughter, no sturdier than her mother, the next queen, depriving me of all possibilities of an advantageous alliance, I find treacherous. There are princesses east of Novgorod who would bring a dowry of Asiatic scope, in amber, furs, and tundra emeralds, to a Western alliance. Hamblet's attachments are not sentimental affairs, but matters for deliberation in the most dispassionate counsels. Never trust an adviser with a marriageable daughter."

Geruthe now put down her brush to turn away from the mirror and say to her husband's face, "It is not any scheme of Corambis's or mine. It is a natural trend we both have noticed, without our encouraging it— Hamblet's fondness for this flower budded in his own court, while he has been mostly absent. On her side, how could she not be fascinated by our royal adolescent, as he

matured into so arresting and expressive a man, preëmi-
nently eligible and yet not spoken for? But she is docile,
and will leave off all hopes, if her father so directs."

"Let him so direct, then. She may be your age of
espousal, but you were no pallid invalid, shrinking into
your father's shadow at a frown."

"When it mattered, I was," Geruthe retorted, her face
growing warm, "as you well remember, having benefited
by my surrender. Ophelia has more mettle and sense and
reserve of passion than you have ever deigned to credit.
She will breed stout progeny, my instinct tells me."

Horvendile looked at her with those phlegmatic pale
eyes that sometimes saw discomfortingly much. "Your
instinct serves your desire, my dear. You read your old
self into her, and would harmonize our only heir to an
imaginary echo of your girlhood. Geruthe, do not seek
in this brittle maid the means to your own late fulfillment, and the conquest of your own son. Tools twist
in our hands when we misapply them, and give us a
wound."

Geruthe set down her brush with a smart click
on the dressing table of briarwood and oak, where
her aids to beauty—scarcely needed, though she was
forty-seven—were arranged: the brush of black-tipped
boar bristles, two ornate combs of ivory, an iron tweezer
for the unwanted hairs that broadened her eyebrows and
crept down her rounded temples, four toothpicks of
which two were ivory and two were gold, some alder
twigs whose ends had been soaked and beaten to form
fibrous brushes for keeping her smile bright and the
toothworm away, a soapstone jar of ground henna pow-

der and another of lapis lazuli with which to smudge her cheeks and eyelids on days of public ceremony, talc to suppress any coarsening ruddiness of complexion, and a "sweet coffer" of fragrant cedar holding perfumed unguents for softening her complexion and easing wrinkles from the skin around her eyes. She spied in her oval metal mirror a face with still a girl's moist fullness, rosy at this moment with anger and startled guilt. She said to Horvendile, "I am merely offering thoughts on the matter that my lord himself raised—how to interest Prince Hamblet in this court and his own royal destiny. I am sorry that my motives appear so twisted, when to me they feel so straightforward and kindly meant."

"Kind advice comes constantly to a king, and he learns to see it all in terms of the bearer's own benefit."

"And reaches the point where suspicion has whittled his heart to the size of the knob of his sceptre," Geruthe responded hotly, "and his own child understandably refuses to come home."

"It is not me he avoids," Horvendile snapped. Then, fearful lest his queen take a hurt from the clear implication that it was she, he said in amends, "It is the—the general climate," giving up on describing a local situation so elusively slack and malodorous.

"What ever happened to Bathsheba?" Fengon asked Geruthe. They were seated in a little-used room of Elsinore, where Fengon's man Sandro, a slender honey-skinned native of Calabria, had persuaded, in very imperfect Danish, an unwilling servant to lay and light a fire. The wood was fresh-chopped ash; the fire smoked; still, the two aristocrats hardly noticed their stinging eyes and cold feet, so intent were they on the intimations each was giving the other, beneath the surface of speech.

In mild panic Geruthe asked, "Bathsheba?"

"The little brown brancher I sent you many years ago, before heading south again. You have forgotten, so accustomed is a queen to gifts from near-strangers."

"Near now, but no stranger ever. I remember. We were not a good match, Bathsheba and I. Her eyes, unseeled, took in too much, and she was forever bating—that is the word?—at bright objects in my chamber as they caught the sun. And she would hurl herself at sounds in the wall, mice or swallows nesting in the chimney, too faint for my ears. I could not reason with her."

"Nor could one with any falcon," Fengon said, in the casual, murmurous voice he used, she had noticed, only with her. Among men and servants he spoke up clearly, even officiously. He had put on weight, his voice volume. "Reason is not their path. In this they are like our deeper selves, over whom the brain would in vain set itself as master."

"A queen in a castle, I discovered, is in poor position to acquire a daily supply of fresh-killed meat. At night her soft but incessant cry—lamenting her loss of freedom, as I imagined it—kept me quite awake. Horvendile's chief falconer took my starving pet into the royal mews, but there existed in those perches an already established order to which the other birds of prey, broken to human use, were not willing to admit our half-wild Bathsheba. The falconer was fearful she would be slaughtered, her throat slashed or her back snapped, in the necessary interval when the birds are unhooded and permitted to use their wings in the mews' high vaults. Thinking that Thord—yes? that was his name?—might take her back, I rode to Lokisheim with a pair of guards, and found only the boy, the pale-faced limping boy—?"

"Ljot," Fengon supplied, his sable eyes swarming with glints, feeding on her every motion and inflection and lineament, so that Geruthe, as she talked, felt her tongue and gestures slowing, as a musician drags his tempo when overly conscious of being listened to. Her skin prickled beneath her heavy diapered surcoat, laced in front, over a blue cotehardie brocaded with silver thread. Could any woman, let alone one of forty-seven summers and no longer lean, withstand the pressure of attention so avid? She was used to being admired but not consumed by eyes like this.

"Little Ljot, yes," Geruthe agreed, hurrying on, through those unsatisfactory events of more than a decade ago, when Fengon's slightly sinister gift had enlisted her in a secret of sorts, though Horvendile had been made aware of his brother's curious present and laughed dismissingly: "As soon give a man a spinning wheel," he had said, "for all the use to be gotten from it!"

She went on, seeking to match the cautious tone of the man she was with, "He said that Thord had fallen sick, of age and the cruel demands of the birds, and your flock had been yielded up, on your instructions in parting, to a dealer from Nødebo in such precious and precarious fowl."

"I did not expect to return soon," Fengon told her. "I had taken a vow."

"What sort of vow?"

"A vow of renunciation."

"What were you renouncing, may I ask?"

"Who better to ask? I was renouncing the sight of you, the sound of you, the faint but maddening scent of you."

She blushed. He had a way of insinuating the unspeakable, yet at her prompting, so she could not fault him. "Surely there was no need," she did protest. "A man is entitled to lend his sister-in-law attendance, if it is done respectfully."

"My thoughts did not exclude respect, but were more than that. They frightened me in their vehemence, their possession of all my waking minutes and then, hideously warped, of my dreams. In my dreams, you were wanton, and I wore a crown. My qualms were perhaps dynastic: I feared that in my love of you and envy of him I might injure my brother."

Geruthe stood, partly in alarm, partly to stir herself, in this cold and smoky room, into warmth. "We must not speak of love."

"No, we must not. Tell me the fate of poor forlorn Bathsheba, too wild for her lady and too tame for nature."

"We took her, Ljot and I, to your field, where I had seen you demonstrate falconry, and set her free."

"Free? But what did freedom mean to her? Death in the talons of a bigger, wilder raptor utterly unspoiled by man's hand." He had stood, too, so as not to loll in the Queen's presence.

"It was not my hand that tamed her," Geruthe said. "We undid the jesses, and at first she flew low, dipping as if she were trailing a creance that would pull her back at will, and then, feeling no tug, she beat herself toward Heaven, and by lifts and lilts explored the breadth of its corridors, yet kept banking obliquely back to be above us, circling quizzically, as if unwilling to give up a connection she had known. She descended it seemed to take my wrist again, but I threw my gauntlet of padded chamois into the tall grass, where she eyed it in flight, as if thinking to retrieve it; but no, then she swooped away mewing, toward the Forest of Gurre in the direction of Elsinore."

"You remember it as if painted on your memory. And did she ever reappear at Elsinore, on your windowsill perhaps?"

"No, but she haunted my thoughts there, as I realized that she had been dear to me, though her value had been eclipsed by the trouble she caused."

"Needing to be fed, you mean."

"And to have her messes swept and scoured and her feathers checked for mites and lice, and the general *worry* of her." Her torso twitched in indignation as if to ring a girdle of bells. "You had burdened me, it seemed, with a representative of yourself, that I dare not neglect, so to keep you alive, whether in the hazards of your travels or in my cherishing memory was unclear."

"The living," allowed Fengon, "make cruel demands." To his manservant he said softly, "*Parta*," and only when the dark young man, who moved with a disquieting docile fluidity that awakened distrust in heavy-footed Danes, had slipped from the chamber did Fengon embrace Geruthe where she stood expectant, indignant and awed by the pit opening up beneath her but afire with the wish to have his lips—curved and cushioned almost like a woman's, and shaping themselves for the pressure of hers in that dense black beard salted with gray—united with hers, so their breaths would each pollute the other's, and the moisture they carried behind their teeth would thrust with their tongues into the other's warm maw. He was solid as a tree, as a rigid young bear, in his diagonally quilted doublet, younger and smaller and firmer than Horvendile. And tasting not of rotting teeth and recent food softened with ale but of living wood, like a mandrake root when as a little girl she chewed and sucked it, excited by the almost-taste, the hint of sweetness coming from underground.

She broke off the embrace. She was panting, an immediate desire slaked but others crowding after it, a chain of shameless petitioners, making her dizzy. "This is sin," she told her partner in it.

He took a dance step backward, his lips twisted by a triumphant amusement. "Not by the laws of love," he rapidly, softly urged. "There are sins against the Church, and sins against nature, which is God's older and purer handiwork. Our sin has been these many years one of denying our natures."

"You think I have loved you?" she asked, not deaf to his presumption, though her body felt swollen and abandoned and longing for his arms as an animal hunted and wounded seeks the safety of the forest.

"I cannot believe—" he began carefully, sensing that she might seize the slightest affront as an excuse to flee his presence forever. "It is a possibly heretical article of my own faith," he began again, "that a creator would not engender so fierce a love in me without allowing in its object the gleam of a response. Can prayer be so futile? You have always received my presence kindly, for all my sins of absence."

Her heart, her hands were fluttering; she felt her life threatened with a large meaning, larger than any since she had been a little princess begging the crumbs of Rodericke's love amid the tumble and alarums of his bawdy court. When you are small, the meanings are large; if in later life you lose childhood's background of assured forgiveness and everlasting rescue, a swerving sense of largeness now and then nevertheless returns. "I can carry on this conversation," she breathed to Fengon, "but not at Elsinore. Look at us, whispering in this cold and smoky nook while your man waits outside, thinking the worst! In these royal precincts nothing goes unobserved, and my own conscience grimaces at the least action that is not queenly. It was better, my dear brother-in-law, when I could cherish the image of you in a place that stretched me to imagine, and remembered fondly how you dared to tease a queen, in a voice pitched like no other she heard, than have you here and face your bold claims."

He slumped to his knees on the stones at her feet, showing her not his face but his bowed head with its grizzled, thick hair and splash of white where a wound had been survived. "I make no claims, Geruthe. I am a beggar sheerly. The truth is simple: I live only in your company. The rest is performance."

"This is not performance?" Geruthe said dryly, brushing his tingling hair with a hand gone cold in the fatality of her commitment. "We must find a better stage—one not borrowed from our king."

"Yes," he said, rising and taking as practical a tone as her own. "My brother is my king, too, and that would gall even if I were not in the base position of desiring his wife."

"Me—so far past my prime? Dear Fengon, did you not meet in those Mediterranean lands younger women to help you forget your plump and aging sister-in-law? One hears that blood runs hot and the nights are thick with the aromas of lemons and flowers, away from our sullen skies." She was trying to move them off that treacherous, leaden ground where they had made, it was plain though unstated, an illicit compact.

He joined her in banter. "They are, and there were such women—women throng every land—but I am a son of the barren heath, and looked in vain for the northern lights in those skies where the stars hung close as fruit. Our lights move elusively, tantalizingly. In comparison, the hot sun and fat moon that encourage the southern races in their lucidity of spirit seemed—what can I say?—vulgar, blatant, coarse—"

"Unsubtle," she provided, laughing at herself and at her harmony with this adorable villain. If the priests keep telling a woman that her lower parts are bad, then she must take a bad man as lover.

Geruthe called Corambis to her on a day when no summons from the King could disturb them. Horvendile was inspecting his troops at the Spodsbjerg garrison, showing himself in full armor, keeping up their morale for the clash, which he said was inevitable, with young Fortinbras and his Norwegian renegades. Geruthe could breathe for a few days. The near presence of her corpulent, war-minded spouse lately had begun to squeeze her lungs; just the thought of him brought a furtive lump to her throat.

The Lord Chamberlain had seemed old to the newly deflowered bride of seventeen when this official, then lithe and just forty, had skied across twelve leagues of fresh snow to confirm the evidence of bloodied sheets; but to the matron of forty-seven he seemed not much older than herself, though his next birthday would be his seventieth, and his unkempt goatee had become quite white. "Dear friend," she began, "you alone in this court have seen through my queenly comportment to the restlessness in my heart."

His moist lower lip slid about thoughtfully before he pronounced, "Many have perhaps glimpsed it, but only I have been privileged to discuss with you a certain mild disquiet."

"Mild grows wild with the years. A modest chafing ends in convulsions."

"Unease, Your Majesty, is the human lot, even for the most exalted. The pampered foot most feels the pinch."

"Don't scold me. I believe you love me," Geruthe said, her hand of its own nervous will dipping toward his knee where he sat in his accustomed three-legged chair, with its pinnacled upright slat that no one could safely lean back on. "And from those we love no shame should shield us." Her hands, having not quite touched him, flitted to indicate the thick stone walls around them. "Elsinore has been a dungeon to me ever since I watched my father die within it. He had pledged me to continue as its mistress. It is not natural to live where we have lived since birth: our spreading roots must snake through heaps of old debris. I had hoped the years would ease my sense of obstruction, as the ears become deaf to a daily repeated sound, be it the cry of rooks or the rattle of fellies on cobblestones; but it has not proven so. My old age approaches. My beauty—which reflected more a simple health than any special grace—is faded, and I have never lived for myself."

"For yourself?" Corambis prompted, rolling his wet lips as if to get the savor of the elusive concept.

"I was my father's daughter, and became the wife of a distracted husband and the mother of a distant son. When, tell, do I serve the person I carry within, the spirit that I cannot stop from hearing, that sought expression with my first bloody cry, burst as I was into the air from my mother's torn loins? When, Corambis? What I need—it really need not shock you—"

The elder statesman tutted fussily, readjusting the extravagant scalloped sleeves of his houppelande. "But, beloved Geruthe, how do any of us define ourselves but in relation to others? There is no unattached free-floating self. By a parallel litany I am the parent of a distant son, Laertes being set upon self-improvement in Paris, and of a very present daughter, present to my concern as a replica of her mother, imperilled by the same otherworldly beauty. I am, to continue this relational way of speaking, Magrit's widower and the obedient servant of my king and, by effortless and proper extension, of his consort, my most excellent queen."

There was a little sting in this laborious protocol, implying the priority of a king over a queen, as if Corambis cagily felt an awkward importunity coming.

She came out with it, then. "I need a place of my own," she told him. "A place to be, however you construe the term, 'by myself,' when my duties permit, away from these crowded halls of Elsinore, yet not so far away that a half-hour's ride will fail to bring me safely back. You once advised me to read and embroider less, and to exert my body in sport more. The place I picture would be embedded in nature, free of the constant witness that attends royalty, where in solitude and salutary idleness I could reclaim the poise and piety that befits a monarch's loving consort."

Corambis listened, head tilted, his lower lip slack, in an attitude of, she felt, rising resistance, as her specific request drew nearer. "Dear old friend," she made herself go on, with a drop into throaty, rapid intimacy that was in part truly impulsive—impulsive affection conjured up by deliberate recall of images from the days when he was still lithe and she lissome—"you know how conscientiously I have trimmed my feelings to suit the demands of Denmark. Is this nation, in all its scattered islands, too small to afford me a single hiding-space? If I cannot have it, then I may be galled to hate this entire polity that hems me in."

Corambis had come fully alert, sensing the danger in her mood. "I cannot imagine Geruthe hating anyone, even those who restrict her liberty. Cheer and generosity have ever been your habit. As a baby rosy in the crib, you would laugh and offer your toys to an onlooker. Of late, my daughter has received from you many benefices of kind attention. She regards you as almost a mother."

"I do love Ophelia, and not merely, as I have been unkindly told, because I fancy my young self in her. I was never so rare as she, nor so shy. I see in her the healing simple whereby my Hamblet can be cured of his coldness, and with him this whole chilly kingdom. But I must save myself," she hurried on, "at least for intervals of privacy more precious than I have been able, I fear, to convey to you."

"You have conveyed enough."

"How strange, that a queen must beg what a peasant wench need only go to the haymow to secure! How foreign this passionate whim of mine must appear to a man, who has only to wrap his cloak about himself, turn his back, and will that the world be banished! You have, Corambis, purchased and improved a mansion on the shore of Gurre Sø, secluded in the Gurre Forest and provided with all the daylight comforts a visitor would need."

"Not a mansion, Your Majesty—by no means a mansion. Hardly a hut, in fact. A disused hunting lodge, rather, built of wood, battens and shakes, the old roof of thatch, the new of slate, built when there was more plentiful game near Elsinore, but thereafter disused, as I say. A curiosity adjoins—an ancient small round tower, of possibly religious purpose, a shrine or chapel erected by rogue anchorites before the great conversion under Harald Bluetooth, or perhaps a religion of an altogether different sort, lakes being often regarded as holy. I have incorporated, rather snugly if I do say so, this relic in the structure overall, filling the gaps in its archaic stonework with modern brick and mortar, refiguring the absent roof in slate and stout rafters, as I said, and supplying the chamber's single gap for a window with the latest and most costly contrivances in fenestration—leaded glazing in the shape of diamonds and discs, and a casement, iron-hinged and levered, that can be latched and securely shuttered or else opened to the air and view of water, dependent on the whim and convenience of the occupant. This fanciful retreat of mine receives small use as long as Elsinore requires my presence, but my conception was that it could be my final home, when the cares of public service have been at long last lifted and I retire to terminal philosophy and holy exercises. It is, as you say, secluded, but near—a quarter of the way to Odinsheim, a half-hour's ride from Elsinore without stretching the horse."

Odinsheim and Lokisheim, both he and she thought. "It is in short a foretaste of Paradise," Geruthe said, "prudently and deservedly prepared in advance of Judgment Day. Indeed, I have seen it, Corambis, one day this autumn when Herda and I took your dear Ophelia riding, to brighten her wan cheeks. She showed it to me with the glee of a girl and a dollhouse—all fitted with the latest contrivances for light and fire and water, yet faithful to the rugged old Norse manner, bristling with antlers and furs, not another dwelling even in sight save for the church whose staved steeple hangs inverted from the lake's far shore, and not a sound but the mutter of wavelets, the chatter of birds, and the furtive traffic of woodland small fry, chasing or being chased. In such a place I could restore my lost composure. My question of you, most dear old friend, is this: Might I not, some two or three occasions in a fortnight, repair there for an afternoon's repose, carrying embroidery or a saint's life to occupy my hands and eyes, or else in idleness laying my hands upon my lap and absorbing goodness from the inhuman lake and woods? I need peace, and Elsinore does not play host to peace. Now that the middle point of my life, however generously we estimate it, has been surely passed, I crave something, let us call it rectitude if not holiness, that will fortify me for what of earth is left. Do grant your queen the brief loan of your haven. Few would know; Herda would come with me, and my personal guard, the most obstinately loyal and mute in our garrison, to put the seal on the solitude and secrecy I seek."

She cut the long speech short there, though her nerves had pushed her tongue on and on, so perilous did her mild lies—containing, like all good lies, some truth—sound in her ears, and so fearful of Corambis's response was she. It irritated her, even, to be at the mercy of her father's and husband's servant, a royal henchman, who in his habitual caution was making her beg unduly for a very modest favor. He should be flattered by this opportunity, though irregular, to serve her.

Corambis eyed her out of his head, squarishly round like a hollowed-out pumpkin, with a stare pinched by the effort to betray no expression. "The King—would he be among those kept ignorant of your whereabouts?"

This entangling venture into deceit was making Geruthe's heart race, annoyingly. Quickly she answered, her white hands darting in multiple disclaimer, "There would be no harm in his knowing, of course, but in honesty I would rather he did not. For him to know would be to plant his presence inescapably in my mind, and I want my mind to be free of even so benign an interloper. In his erratic solicitude for me he might come visiting, all those rattling, caparisoned horses, at the moment when I was least attuned to his uxorious mood. This all sounds a bit heartless, I know, but if you reflect on your joyous years with Magrit you might recall how marriage must flow through intervals of privacy; otherwise a sludge of resentments never has time to clear."

"Your departures and returns could not but be observed at the castle. There would be speculation."

"Well, if the King were to discover these harmless retreats of mine, he would be told, correctly, that they were spiritual exercises, improving meditations. I who once wasted my afternoons dreaming through idle romances involving knights and scaly monsters will bring instead vellum-bound copies of the Gospels, or the Epistles, or else edified commentaries, such as our Bishop propagates from Roskilde. It is true, good Corambis, and none bore closer witness than you, that my father's court was indifferently pious, and my instruction in the mysteries of Christ was considerably neglected. I support the Creed, like all respectable Danes, but can scarcely spell out its articles. Christ died and was raised, thus overturning nature, fallen since Adam; but nature remains without and within us. How could my king, whose faith runs so much deeper than mine own, and whose overarching project is to render the nation he rules more truly Christian, object if I seek, in seclusion, to refine my knowledge of holiness?"

Corambis did not like Horvendile and never had, and he *did* like her: Geruthe's advantage lay with these intuitions, borne out by a thousand small incidents and sensations accumulated in her many days within the walls of Elsinore.

"He would not," the Lord Chamberlain decided, and, with a slippery brief smile, which made his goatee bob, and an awkward jerky bow attempted without rising, so that the chair creaked, he went on, "nor can I deny my queen recourse to my humble shelter, if such a condescension into the forested wild is what her spirit craves."

"I crave it, though fearfully, as a foray into spaces of myself yet blank. I am timid, but too advanced in age not to go forward."

"In a selfless cause," he reminded her. "A campaign for your very soul. I will advise the man and wife who from their nearby cottage keep watch over my lodge on Gurre

Sø that the Queen is welcome to come and go and that her visits should be undisturbed."

"The Queen is most grateful and will search for a way to express her pleasure," she said.

But the old politician would not let her off so cheaply. "All blessings flow from the throne to its servants," he said. "Nothing in my keeping could be denied to you. But yet I confess this drawback: for one in my position, to keep a secret from the King is treason, the most capital of crimes."

There was truth in this, and, though she was regally accustomed to having many fates bound up with hers, her heart quailed at taking the old man with her into treachery. He had not her grievances, nor her ardor. "A domestic secret merely," she lightly told him. "You are my co-conspirator in a plot to make me a better wife, a wiser consort."

Corambis sighed and shifted his weight once more, adjusting his conical green hat to align with the dissatisfied tilt of his head. He put his hands on the chair arms as if to push off and rise; his hands looked alarmingly withered, though the middle of him still appeared plump. "I do it for you as you *were*," he confessed to her, weary of circumspection. "You were so buoyant a lass, to be tied to that plumb weight."

Horvendile, the blond beast who came courting in his burgundy cloak and shirt of mail, a plumb weight? She defended him: "He loves me still, I think."

"In due portion, not a pennyweight more," Corambis said, seeing more clearly than she the course they were on, and not wishing to muddy the picture. Blinking at the future, he sighed. "When a king and queen disagree, it puts their advisers' heads near the block."

"I would not have you risk yourself for my sake," Geruthe lied.

He slumped back into the ill-fitting chair. "Even advisers cannot always be slaves to good advice. 'Neither a borrower nor a lender be,' it is said, yet life is a tangle of payments and defaults; it ensnares us all into debt. I suspect that our king would like to see me dismissed, which renders my risk either greater or less than otherwise— quite which, I cannot judge. But I think my stake, measured in years of royal favor remaining, is small and dwindling."

"You are the father of a future queen," Geruthe assured him. "As such, you are scarcely dismissable."

"Ah, don't push that chance too hard, milady. Ophelia is still a child; she is apt to yield what cannot be recovered, getting nothing for it but contempt. Hamblet is arrogant, and walks on a longer tether than she, and enjoys using the full length of it. I fear he does not value my angel as do you and I."

It was with difficulty that Geruthe gave her attention to this thread of the plot, she was so intent on her own, so enraptured by the prize she had won. She had secured a place away from Elsinore. And spring was coming. The willow buds were long and a living yellow, and those of the oaks grew ruddy and fat.

"Tell me about Byzantium," she bade Fengon at their first assignation. As winter receded, she had established her use of Corambis's lakeside lodge, accepting from horseback the curtsies of the old woman in her thatched cottage, while her lame-legged husband—he had been a woodsman; the ax had slipped—scuttled along the path to start the fires burning. Her two mute guardsmen would wait in the dirt-floored entry room, with a sluggish peat blaze to warm their hands and feet by. Herda sat in a sunken stone-floored chamber, the lodge hearthroom, its central hearth big enough to spit a boar and a smoke vent at the roof's peak opened and closed with a long pole, and benches against the walls that could have served huntsmen as beds. Geruthe took refuge two rooms away—beyond the high-ceilinged banquet hall adorned with stag antlers and stretched bearskins, the great snarling skulls still attached, down a low-roofed newly built passage, and up six steps—in the old round tower. This bedchamber's one glazed casement window, lancet in shape, opened on a curtain of greenery. Long-needled larches were mixed with faster-growing trees whose spreading leaves would, if unchecked by a woodsman, smother them. The lake glittered through the leaves. A small fireplace, rimmed with a band of blue-tinged tiles from Friesland, was vented by a flue built into the outside wall in the newest fashion, but Geruthe preferred to be warmed by standing braziers filled with glowing coals, one on either side of her as she sat at her embroidery frame or slowly turned the bright parchment pages of Gospels in recalcitrant Latin.

Small inked men in pink-and-blue robes, with large fish-shaped eyes and stiff little minnow-mouths, offered, at each dotted and knotted initial, to animate the holy

texts, along with animals of unreal coloring and fantastic form, and winged angels bringing miniature scrolls
to mankind, or blowing gilded horns, or lifting two
fore-fingers in dire wide-eyed warning; she was happy to
let a vague sense of glad tidings and remote heavenly
organization arise from the pages much as the braziers
emanated heat at her elbows. When she became too
warm, she moved about the room with its canopied
feather bed, touching the luxuries of smooth tile and
marble mantel and tin candle-sconce and leaded glass—
the old widower's concupiscence expressed in gadgetry.
Bubbles in the diamond-shaped panes of glass made the
tree trunks waver and bend. She listened to a mouse
scurry and her heart flutter as she tried to gauge the
depth of the betrayal she was plotting. Birdsong outside
the window, quickening as the April light signalled to the
feathered tribe the approach of nesting season, soothed
Geruthe with nature's essential innocence. And yet how
were these creatures rewarded for their innocence? With
death the next season, when the falcon stoops, or snow
covers the seedy grasses.

Carefully she had revealed to Fengon, in their cramped
and snatched but gatheringly pointed exchanges in stolen
corners of vast, formal, echoing Elsinore, the existence
of her retreat, and then its whereabouts, and then, some
days ago, a day, today, when she would be there alone but
for her servants and not averse to a visit from him, if he
could contrive secrecy. The lancet window's hinged casement swung outward, and when wide open it was not too
narrow to admit a man, one agile enough to raise himself

to the sill. The sill was a man's height and half again off the ground. Emblematically, a venerable vine, with profuse heart-shaped leaves, had gripped the large old stones so securely that the masons when renovating, fearing its removal would tumble all down, had merely trimmed its branches and worked around its crooked trunk; stubbornly flourishing, it offered a slippery ladder, affording boot-tips a scant purchase. Fengon, having tethered his horse out of sight and accepted a boost from Sandro, clung and struggled upwards grunting and smirking at such middle-aged heaving: Geruthe had to hurry and pull at one arm when it seemed he was stuck midway through the window, the heaviness of his fifty-nine years exactly balanced against his muscular will. Thus with her help he arrived erect and mussed in the room, his wolfish teeth sheepishly grinning in his speckled oval beard.

Seeing her backed away, having helped him in but startled by the sudden possibility of his rough embrace, he contented himself with a courtly, taming kiss that barely grazed the back of her trembling white hand. Now, still lightly panting, seated with her in the overlapping rings of heat emitted by the twin braziers, he sought, as they hesitated at the edge of the incestuous crime yawning at their feet, to obey her command. Talking not directly to the purpose was one of the diplomatic arts he had learned.

"It is a land much like Denmark," he answered, "composed of islands, though the islands of Byzantium are shuffled by the fortunes of war, which for centuries have been favoring her enemies—the Genoans, the Venetians, the Franks, the Nicaeans, the Bulgarians, the Georgians, the Sultans of Seljuk, the Alans and the Cumans, the Khans of Persia, the Mamlukes of Egypt. Its once-vast empire is ground small between the followers of Mahomet, who consider the Byzantines cursed infidels, and the Christians loyal to the Pope in Rome, who consider them damned heretics. For all that, there is a metropolitan excitement to Constantinople which capitals less bedevilled lack. It is the greatest city in the world, unless China holds its compare. The court has a pomp, a hieratic glitter, that none other in Europe can equal. It is the pivot point, Constantinople, where Asia meets Europe, and black Africa impinges upon the white wastes that feed the Volga and the Don. Everybody comes there, Geruthe, all the world mingling—there are even, I was astonished to discover, Danes. Our Viking forebears made their way down the tumultuous rapids of the Dneiper with their battle-axes and amber and furs; some survived to father blue-eyed Greeks. Danes, Swedes, Norwegians, and English compose the Emperor's Varangian Guard, and are much esteemed for their brute pugnacity. A special graveyard exists for us, near the Adrianople Gate. I spent many a good hour bringing my compatriots up to date, in a language they had all but forgotten how to speak. To the old Norsemen, Constantinople was Miklagard, the fairy city, where dreams were reality. The Byzantines, in a mirroring fantasy, call Denmark Brittia and say that a wall divides the country in two parts: one side is healthy and happy, and the other is pestilential and full of snakes. This better describes their own divided natures; they are both pious and wicked in the extreme. They are cruel as children are cruel, in unfeeling innocence. Their version of Christian worship is only outward mummery, greatly prolonged; the priests perform the miracle of transubstantiation behind an ornamented screen, and then gobble up all the bread themselves. The people are darker than we, but only by a tinge, and they have a glossy blackness of hair beside which mine is dull. My little spot of white they took as a sign of magical powers. They are inordinately fond of garlic, baths, and castration."

"Fengon, you speak of your social congress with the Danish community, but did you make no contact with, say, a Greek woman keen to bear a blue-eyed child?"

He waved her jealous probe away, as unworthy of his heart's queen. "Communication was erratic. Their rulers and priests—often the same men—speak of course some Latin as well as Greek, a more liquid and running tongue. The lower orders, dealing with a foreigner, make do in a patchwork of phrases taken from French and Italian and even some German, though they think that Hungary is a Germanic nation, and Spain a caliphate, neither of which absurdity is entirely wrong. The Jewish and Lebanese merchants that pour through Constantinople have extensive linguistic skills, as do the prostitutes, who constitute a large and thriving class. The government in its cynical debasement exacts an eighth of this charming sisterhood's earnings for its coffers."

Geruthe went rigid; if at this moment she could have called upon her beloved Horvendile to slay this insolent mocker, lazing in his whorish recollections, she would have.

"So I was informed by hearsay," Fengon went on smoothly. "Myself, I was pledged to an unattainable lady, and content to be chaste in her service. It was not difficult to suppress craving in a realm so given to, on the one hand, disgusting excess and, on the other, asceticism and self-torture. Monasteries are built upon the remotest crags and islets, to escape the world's temptations, and yet for some monks the isolation and privation of such places is not enough, and they corrupt one another with frequent sodomy. Holy men are admired in proportion to the cruelty they inflict upon themselves. They condemn their bodies to sleeplessness, to standing upright for days on end; they jubilantly starve their sinful bellies; they mount pillars and live atop them for decades. They show more care for the worms that live in their wounds than for their own tormented flesh. In their mania for purity they live in holes, like St. Joannikos, or dwell in swamps as food for mosquitoes, like St. Makarios. There are hesychasts, who sincerely expect the divine light to come pouring forth from their navels."

Geruthe tittered in surprise; Fengon was encouraged to go on with his incredible tale: "For a time, Geruthe, their church turned against its own icons, and ripped marvellous mosaics from the walls and domes of its basilicas, and condemned to death those faithful who harbored in their homes images of Christ and His blessed mother. Their churches, unlike our own, with their clean smells of cedarwood and mistletoe, stank of sickly incense, of rancid chrism and the drippings of votive lamps. Lunatics and saints were indistinguishable in Byzantium, as were bishops and assassins—their morbid religiosity made me long for the simplicity of our fresher, barer faith, which deals less with outer show than with inner purity."

"I wonder you and I dare talk of purity."

Fengon's teeth flashed their tawny pallor. The lower were irregularly crowded, and his canines were sharp. "Why not? Is not this encounter chaste? Has our conversation at any point held even a hint of adultery? If it has, may I cut off my tongue, as a starter. You receive me through so strait a gate"—he indicated the lancet window—"I could not bring a single Greek gift."

"Have you gifts for me?" What a child she still was, she noticed of herself, so quickly curious as to what material objects might reveal of his thoughts of her in so far and fantastic a land. Outside the window, birds chirped in their version of abrupt and fluting Danish, and buttons of pale-green leaf, budded but yesterday, dotted the cool air darkened by larches. This man, for all the devious unknowns about him, brought her home to herself. No failing she displayed to him would meet the distracted frown her husband wore when she claimed his notice. Rodericke's paternal approval had been reborn. The focus in which Fengon held her burned and soothed at once.

He laughed at her innocent avidity and said, "If I visit

you again, perhaps I may use the front door, as did my servant Sandro, who sits down below with your Herda, sharing cakes and cider and a conspiratorial silence."

She laughed in turn. "Can you see through walls? Did you truly become a magician in Byzantium?"

"Not a magician, but a—a cosmopolite, a connoisseur of human nature. I have lived where men of every race and disposition mingle, and all is tacitly permitted. The *dunatos*, the powerful ones, live in a luxury of porphyry and jasper while two steps from their gilded doors those without a home huddle and starve, the mother dying as the infant sucks on nothingness. Extremes of piety and cruelty meet there in a bloody mist. They punish adultery by cutting off the lady's pert nose, after which she enters a nunnery, which in turn may be a brothel, so widespread is the holy vocation. When an emperor is deposed, which happens not infrequently, the new one, as if performing a courtesy, gouges out the eyes of his predecessor, the better to prepare him for the next world, and to remove him from the politics of this. Yet they are far from brutes, the Byzantines. The pleasures of battle seem to them unsavory. They prefer to buy off their enemies, or to hire others from less civilized lands to fight them. Their favorite method of private murder is poison, which their apothecaries have refined to a high art. These eastern Romans have severed conscience from religion, which frees them to move in their silks as in a pond overstocked with eels, one across another, without friction of the abrasive, hidebound kind so common here in the north, to which they have given the pretty name of Thule."

She shuddered. "I am glad, nevertheless, that it was you who went, and not I."

"They would have greatly esteemed you. Red-haired slaves bring twice what the less fair do."

"Do you miss them terribly, these warm-water eels? I fear you must be impatient with our frozen ways."

"I am *of* you, Geruthe, a Dane to the bone. None but one lady answers to my inner ideal. You are my *haghia sophia*, my holy wisdom."

"Wisdom, sir, or folly?" She smiled, showing the gap between her front teeth.

"In Constantinople," he explained, "there are many religious currents, and one holds that to each man belongs a Form of Light, which is his own spirit remained in Heaven, far from the hellish prison of matter all around us. At death his Form of Light will greet him with a kiss, a Kiss of Love so-called, reënacted in some heretical sects, to the horror of the strictly orthodox. She is his personal savior, manifesting Sophia Maria, the feminine principle of divinity. Call it high-flown if you will, I do believe you are such to me."

Geruthe blushed at the heat of so inflamed a phrasing of his attraction. "It is high-flown to the point of blasphemy; it puts nature in altogether too extravagant a gown."

"I recognize my feelings exactly in it. On our earthly plane, my devotion, I know, is absurd. You are a woman, and many exist, as I allowed a minute ago."

She answered in offended kind. "You would theologize me out of my real existence. I would rather have the material gifts," she told him, almost angrily, on a queen's dignity, "that you say you possess but could not scrape through the window. Next time, use the door, as your servant has done. We are too old for puppy love's acrobatics. Let Corambis's haven be ours for the odd hour, for what conversations we wish, without timorous skulking. Those who know of it are our collaborators, and the risks of collaboration bind them to silence."

"I fear not for myself," Fengon said, his words slowed as if each one must meet a test of honesty. "I have courted danger these years, giving God the option of ridding the world of my disruptive passion. This love was not dangerous when you were out of reach, my *amors de terra lonhdana*. But now that you are near, your face and gestures fitting as a key a lock my fanatically cherished memory of them, I fear for us both. I fear for the throne, and for Denmark."

"You fear too much, it may be, and dream too hard. Great estates have rarely turned on the sleight of a lady's favor. You call ethereal what in truth we share with all animals. I believe we have had this debate before, whether love is skyey or earthen. I am earthy, and dying to hold and weigh the gifts you say you have brought, from this Miklagard I will never see, a poor pale lady of Thule."

Fengon gathered that she would grant him naught but this ultimatum today, and he bowed in leaving. Sandro had not expected him to emerge so soon, or to leave by way of the passage into the hearth-room, for he looked up startled from the depths of a dialogue between himself and Herda. She was twice his age, but with traces still of comeliness. By the great central bed of embers they huddled over unglazed cups of mulled cider. They were working out a language; Sandro filled in his gaps of Danish with supple gestures that left her blinking.

"*Una regina*," Fengon told him in answer to the question in his face as they left, "*non è una gallina.*"

His first gift, brought the week following, when the buds of the maples and alders had gone from a buttonlike solidity to the particulate leafiness of tiny cabbages, was a cloisonné pendant in the form of a peacock, the spread tail a fan in whose center the neck and body of shimmering blue stood out against the proud spread of green feathers eyed in yellow and black. Each segment of enamel was outlined in gold finer than thread, even to the tiny chips of white and red, green and gray that gave anatomy to the profiled head with its downcurved beak. The maker of so fine a thing must soon have gone blind; his blindness was part of its worth. "You always give me birds," Geruthe said, then remembered that the first such present, the pair of pied linnets, had come from Horvendile.

"The peacock," he explained, "is their symbol of immortality. One sees these fowl often in the courtyards, dragging their splendid feathers in the dust, stretching their iridescent necks to make their maddening cry, more like that of a soul in torment than of an emblem of Paradise."

"It is very beautiful, and heavy." She lifted it, the pendant and its gold chain, which was so fine it slithered like a trickle of liquid into her pink palm.

"See if it feels so around your neck. May I put it on you?"

Geruthe hesitated, then bowed her head and let him take this liberty. His fingers as he did so stroked her hair, finest-spun and palest at the nape of her neck, where his fingers toyed with the chain's catch. His lips, ruddy and shapely, were inches from her eyes as he felt for the fit. Finding it, his hands lifted, but his mouth did not move back. Each black hair of his mustache had an enamelled lustre. A feather of his breath, smelling of cloves brought from afar, brushed her nostrils. She lifted a finger to touch his fringed lips, to create there a tingle to mirror that which she had felt at the back of her neck. The weight of the pendant tugged there with a little cool strip of pressure. Their two bodies, proximate, felt huge to her, as if made up of tiny whirling microcosms, each part and filament of them as precious as the enamel fragments of the immortal peacock. The chill at the back of her neck pushed her to seek the warmth of his lips, where her fingertips had briefly explored.

She and Fengon kissed, but not as avidly, as moistly, as they had in Elsinore. Here, in their own, more modest castle, they advanced with more caution, without the King's paternal protection, attempting to domesticate the outrage their bodies were plotting. Geruthe felt guilt more keenly, since she was the married one, and yet an old sense of outrage rose up to meet and overpower her qualms for the length of the kiss and its several less heated, more practiced successors, until, weary of the revolution within, she pulled back, and begged Fengon for conversation.

But Byzantium and all of Europe south of Slesvig was becoming, each day he lingered in Denmark, less distinct to him, his travels reducing in his mind to an impatient temper foreign to stolid Danes, an edgy hardness waiting inside him like a sheathed sword. Geruthe worked at teasing his youthful past from him—the Jutland boyhood, the early raids at Horvendile's side, his education, ragged and by rote, at the hands of priests—and talked then of herself, gaily, with a reckless frankness, remembering her grievances against father, husband, and son as if they were all episodes of an amusing history belonging to another woman. Fengon heard in her gaiety a new resolve, to go ahead, with a resilient hardness of her own. She was drunk, it seemed to him, on anticipation, and steeled against her own guilt.

From Sandro's discreet demeanor, on the ride back to Lokisheim, his visit with the Queen had been closer to the proper duration.

Her second gift, brought in a week when the buds were loosening enough to fill the woods with a yellow-green fog, was a chalice, silver so thinly worked it could cut a lip, only the stem bejewelled, but thickly so, with knobs of green chrysoprase, rose quartz, and reddish-brown carnelian. The bowl of the goblet was incised with lacy designs that inspection revealed to be trees, trees more symmetrical than trees could be and spiralling inward toward a foliate impossibility in which snakes were nested, snakes and apples, and birds too large for the linear branches upon which they symmetrically rested. Their eyes were ringed, their beaks tangent to triangular bunches of what she guessed were grapes.

On the cup's other side, opposite this laden and inter-twining tree, symmetrical beasts posed beside a pillar topped by a cross, a cross whose forked ends flared out-ward into lines that enclosed a kind of star. Crouched on either side of the pillar as if posed before a mirror, the beasts were horses in body except that the feet were not hooved but taloned, too long-toed to be lions' paws. The forelegs at their shoulders broadened upward into feath-ered wings, and the faces, seen frontally, were not horses' heads or lions' but those of smiling women, women wearing bangs and on their thin necks necklaces whose square elements echoed the segmented locks of the bangs. And the faces of these women—perhaps they were children—were beautiful and serene. "Are these phoenixes?" Geruthe asked, emerging from her trance of inspection to discover that Fengon's face was beside hers, sharing the inspection, for he had purchased this gift long ago and had half forgotten its Byzantine details.

"Something of the sort," he said. His voice so close to her ear bore its own scratchy, moist breath-marks, a texture from within, a rustle of uncertainty. "The Greek word is *chimaira*—from 'she-goat,' but meaning a she-monster, put together of the parts of sundry animals." His hand, she realized, was resting on her waist, the side away from him, his touch no heavier than another layer of cloth. In the sudden warmth of the April day she had discarded her dark wool mantle, leaving only a gold-embroidered bliaut covering her chemise of white linen. She did not move away or reveal that she knew she was being touched.

"And the precious stones," she said, caressing their lumpy smoothness, rimmed in pronged silver settings. "Another extravagant mixture. So thick and encrusted a stem, on so fine and easily dented a cup. It makes the products of even our most skillful Danish smiths seem coarse." It reminded her, in its lumpy heft, of something she had often handled, with mixed emotions, distaste and dread yielding to amusement and wonder.

"What I liked about it," said Fengon, in his soft, on-running voice, "and what made me think of you, years ago in a market in Thessaloniki, was its cheerfulness, a rounded good humor about it—the faces of the chimeras reminded me of you, two of you."

Light from the lancet window clarified the incised lines. Yes, she thought, the smiling faces were not unlike the plump face she saw in her oval metal mirror each day, though she did not wear her hair in Attic bangs but pulled back in coiled braids. Two of her, for two brothers—the fancy gave rise to the unease, the foreboding, that she sought each day to keep down, like a surge of nausea. "We should drink together from this gorgeous gift," she decreed. "Perhaps Sandro and Herda are not too wrapped in discussion to fetch us a flagon of Rhenish wine. Corambis keeps a cask in his larder; he has laid in provisions here for a siege. Horvendile speaks of him more and more as a rascal, looking only to his own prosperity." She regretted pronouncing her husband's name, though Fengon had known it, and the man it designated, twice as long as she.

"The Hammer is never altogether wrong," he said,

releasing her from his touch and dancing away in that frisky, foreign way he had. "Were I Corambis, I too would be looking to my own security. If we define 'rascal' thus, few can dodge the epithet. Wine by all means, though we have but one cup. Is it enough?"

"The pantry holds dozens."

"But this one is ours. Yours, since I gave it to you, with my pledged adoration." He ventured from their covert chamber, and in time Herda, her face composed in the mask of service, brought them not only a pottery flagon on a lindenwood tray but bread and cheese. Fengon used the dagger at his belt to make portions for them. The wine was thick and sweet, and under its influence, drinking first from opposite sides and then from the same of the heavy-stemmed cup, they could not help rubbing against each other, and fell to the bed, where, removing no clothes, they groped for sensitive flesh while exchanging reechy kisses, their mouths sour with wine, tainted with cheese, but for all that sweet, deeply so; it was as if two great angelic funnels were pouring through their joined lips the long-dammed contents of their souls, all the wounds in need of healing, all the comforts until now unbestowed. They became in their clothes sweaty and pink. His hands sought her loins, her breasts through the embroidered bliaut, with its welts of thread, that sheathed her from neck to heels. A ridge of dew appeared on Geruthe's upper lip, which bore a transparent down he had never noticed before; her hand sought below his belted velvet tunic the baubly stalk his gift had reminded her fingers of. But for all this compulsive ardor, these swathed caresses and stifled groans, the hissing and broken murmurs, the spiritual undertaking was too great to be consummated today. The weight of fatality was too heavy for their mere flesh.

On the morrow she accompanied the King to Skåne, that band of distant purple beyond the sullen Sund. A Danish land since the dark age when the Jutes and Angles divided the great peninsula now ruled from Elsinore, Skåne, with Halland and Blekinge, bordered the territories of the Swedish king, who coveted Skåne's rich soil and herring harvest. Horvendile felt it politic to exhibit the royal presence there. He and his queen paid state visits to Lund, where the Archbishop mounted a three-day banquet, and to Dalby, where the Bishop organized a state procession around the city walls, led by a host of saints' bones in individual reliquaries. Geruthe and Horvendile paid a patriotic visit to the battlefield of Fotevig, where over a century ago Erik the Memorable had decisively defeated Niels and his son Magnus, who had treacherously murdered Duke Knud the Breadgiver, conqueror of the Wends, in Haraldsted Wood. Magnus fell at Fotevig together with no fewer than five bishops. Erik's victory had been aided by three hundred German armored knights hired for the occasion, a technological innovation which at a blow rendered popular levies upon the peasantry obsolete.

Fengon's freelance profession, Geruthe reflected, had been born here. In Horvendile's constant company, she found her liaison with his brother increasingly dreamlike. Horvendile was always at his best when travelling, being fêted and paraded, charming other dignitaries with his fattened Nordic handsomeness. The cheering populace lined their routes, and threw spring flowers—daffodils, apple blossoms—under the hooves of their snorting steeds, who were spooked by the tumult.

A byproduct of his buoyant mood was a more devoted attention to his queen. Their lovemaking resumed, in the canopied beds of their ecclesiastical hosts, as if their young marriage had never grown jaded and old. Her husband was bulkier than Fengon, his body not so wiry and keen in her arms, his beard less thick and stiff, but he was *good*, a dutiful king and husband, and on both counts *hers*, her king, her husband, her conqueror. Satisfactorily he hammered her. She had only to hold still, like the faithful runestone King Gorm had erected to Tyra, Denmark's glory, and fair fortune and renown would come to her. Her incestuous flirtation with Fengon, seen from a distance, appalled her. How perilously close she had come to falling! As soon as she returned, she would tell him, gently but unmistakably, that their meetings must come to an end. Her impatience to do so, to rid herself of imminent (how could she have come so close!) disgrace, gave her insomnia in Skåne.

But after her return to Elsinore, Fengon was rarely in attendance, and when he did come his business was with his brother and the court. Geruthe's impulse of renunciation was replaced by a painful sensation of having been herself renounced. Her cheeks burned in shame to think back upon the avowals she had urged into his ear, and their delving kisses, and her heat within her clothes, whose embrace had alone held her from a ruinous surrender.

A week had passed after her return when Corambis

took her aside into a little recess of the long, pillared, unevenly paved corridor on the way to the chapel. "The excursion to Skåne has put a new gloss upon my queen's mien," he observed, but tentatively, as if willing to be contradicted. They had their secret between them, which freighted their words with danger.

"It was a relief to get away from Elsinore and its petty intrigues," she said, rather loftily. "The King shone to glorious advantage. The people over there adored him."

"The sun rises in the east," Corambis said. His red-rimmed eyes, their lids yellow and loose, twinkled as if he had said something witty. She wondered how senile he was becoming: that absurd outdated sugarloaf hat, that houppelande with its trailing scalloped sleeves. She understood how Horvendile might feel: get rid of the gabby old baggage.

"The people are so trusting and loving," she said. "One forgets, sometimes, whom one is ruling. It lifts the heart to see them."

"Without forgetfulness, milady, life would be intolerable. All that we have ever felt or known would come crowding in upon us, like rags stuffed into a bag, as they say happens to unfortunates in the moment of drowning. It is averred that it is a painless death, but only the drowned could tell us with assurance, and they are silent, being so. That is, drowned." He waited, head cocked and hat with it, to see what she might make of such assorted wisdom.

"I will endeavor not to drown," she stated coolly. He was anxious, she could sense, to pick up the trail of their shared secret and bygone collusion.

"All Denmark wishes you to swim, none more fervently than I. It gladdens my cloudy old sight to see Rodericke's daughter enjoy the love and esteem to which her proud blood entitles her. You have taken less joy in the throne, as we have previously discussed, than could be imagined by those multitudes who do not sit upon it."

"We have had many discussions, on this matter or that, in our long acquaintance."

"Indeed, and I beg forgiveness if I seem to thrust one more upon you. But, speaking of forgetfulness, as I believe we just were, unless I forget, a mutual friend of ours wonders whether or not he has been, in the stimuli and exaltations of your travels, forgotten."

"He stays at Lokisheim, and seems himself forgetful."

Corambis, last living link to her father's dishevelled court, and safeguard of her childish identity, now seemed to be leading her astray, tugging her back to what she had resolved to put behind her. "He is far from forgetful, but respectful of your wishes."

"My wish—" She could not quite entrust to this elderly intermediary words of severance that Fengon deserved to hear from her own lips.

Corambis's tongue moved quickly into her pause. "He has a third gift to deliver, he bade me remind you. It is his last, and if you deign to receive it, it will spell quits to his giving, and to his heretical leanings, whatever that might mean. The phrase is his."

"My wish, I started to say, is to avail myself no more of your quiet lodge by Gurre Sø, now that the weather is pleasant enough to offer retreat out of doors. Your queen is most grateful for your permissive hospitality. I recovered a measure of contentment and resignation in my virtual solitude."

Yet her heart beat at the picture of Fengon alone with her there, where the secluded lake gleamed to its far inverting shore, reflecting the sky like a great oval salver.

"He asked me to beg you to name a day," Corambis insisted gently, with a courtier's reluctance to disturb royal equanimity.

Haughty, wishing this pander and his pathetic daughter banished from her arrangements, Geruthe named the next day.

The woods around them were freshly but fully leafed. A steady warm drizzle further reduced visibility. The far side of the lake with its church could not be seen. The month had changed from April to May. The guards who rode with her—stolid on the way, looser and even jolly on the way back, with the ale absorbed while waiting through her rendezvous—seemed solemn and tense today, as if aware of a decisive point reached. Herda, marking this long-deferred resumption of the picnic habit, had packed an ample lunch—enough cheese and bread and salt meat and dried fruit for six—and the sight of the bright osier basket so heavily laden lightened the whole adventure somehow, making it seem less terminal than Geruthe had conceived it. We eat, we ride, we experience the days in their tones of weather, we love, we marry, we encounter life in each of its God-ordained stages, no plague or accident cutting it short—life is part of nature, its beginning impossible to recall and its ending not to be contemplated outside of church, the home of last things.

Fengon and Sandro were late, as they had never been before, as if putting off an adverse verdict. When they came, they were soaked by the nine leagues from Lokisheim. Fengon distractedly explained, "We had to be careful, where the road was rocky, the horses didn't slip on the wet stones." He knew he had lost ground. Alone with her in their corner room, he twitched with nervous energy, and shivered in his soaked cloak. He smelled of wet wool, wet leather, wet horse. The fire the lame caretaker had built had nearly died in the delay; together they worked at reviving it. Fengon laid too many logs too close; Rodericke had told Geruthe as a girl, one night as she sat drowsy in his lap after dinner, that a fire was a creature that needed like all others to breathe. Their interview today would be short; there would not be time for the brazier coals to heat.

The log fire poked into a reluctant revival, Fengon stood and said accusingly, "You enjoyed Skåne."

"Women enjoy travel. It is a pity, since we are rarely invited."

"Horvendile was a satisfying companion."

"Yes, Fengon. Pomp is his element, and his happiness overflowed onto me."

"I fear that those of us you left behind gave you little reason to return."

She had to smile, for all her grim resolve, at this

bearded man's boyish sulk. "I had, for reason, the third gift you promised me. From your temper, you would as soon save it for another, who gratifies you more."

"You gratify me all too well, as I believe I have persuaded you. But my inkling today is that it would be presenting a vain bribe to my executioner."

Outside the lancet window the soft rain pattered from shelf to shelf of fresh greenery. Never had they felt so sealed in. Fengon was unexpectedly vivid to her—his soaked odor, his clever face tanned with spring's windy sun, his nervous, offended warmth. Horvendile and the ecclesiastical pageants of Skåne seemed far at her back. Geruthe had noticed before how hard it was to hold one man in mind while confronting another.

She told him, lightly, "All mortals are mounting the gallows steps, but how near to the top we have come only God knows. Your inkling characterizes me unkindly. As soon call me your rescuer. We know equally well the height of the fall we might take. To banish you from these private audiences would be but to reinforce your own wise action when you last banished yourself from Denmark, a dozen years ago."

"I was well short of fifty then, and am now nearing sixty. I thought to shake your spell, but instead it strengthened and I have weakened. My life runs low on chances. But have no mercy on me. The Queen must save herself; her whim is justice, her word is my law."

Geruthe laughed, at her fickle, fluttering feelings as much as at Fengon's chastising gravity. He looked monkish in his soggy hood. "Take off your stinking cloak, at least," she commanded him. "Did you bring my final present in it?"

"Bundled dry against my breast," he said. Removing his cloak, he spread out for her on the bed a long woman's tunic woven of interlocking and wavering peacock colors, green and blue and yellow spiced with black and red specks, the fabric more flexible than skin itself, though stiffened at the collar and sleeve-ends and hem with rows of tiny sewn pearls. Its threads caught the light as if faceted. "This kind of cloth is novel in Denmark," Fengon explained. "Silk. The thread is secreted by horned green worms fed only on mulberry leaves. The eggs and seeds, the legend goes, were once smuggled out of China by Persian friars in their hollow staffs, and thus to Byzantium. The cocoons the worms spin, for a blind moth that lives but a few days, are boiled and picked apart by children's fingers, and then old women braid the filaments into yarn, woven in turn into patterns as miraculous as that which you see, to image forth the bejewelled glory of Heaven."

Geruthe touched the shimmering cloth, and in that touch was her undoing. "I should put it on," she said.

"Not so your husband will see it, for he would know it is no item of northern manufacture."

"I should put it on now, for its giver to appraise. Stand there." She wondered at her tone of command. She had mounted to an eminence of abandon. The rain thickened to a torrent outside and the room dimmed, but for the shuddering glow of the revived fire. Its heat coated Geruthe's skin as she shed her own damp cloak, and the sleeveless surcoat, and her long plain tunic with its flow-

ing sleeves, and the white cotte beneath that, leaving
only a linen chemise, in which she shivered. Fine drops
ricocheting from the stone sill of the window behind her,
its casement left ajar, pricked her bared skin. The fire's
heat on her arms and shoulders felt like an angelically
thin armor. Again she was reminded of something from a
far corner of her life—a wifely memory faintly tasting of
humiliation. The Byzantine tunic, stiff where those
bands were knobbed with pearls, shrouded her head for a
rustling instant, in which the sound of the rain overhead
on the slates merged with the amplified rush of blood in
her ears. Then, her head restored to air and light, she
posed in the splendid sheath of silk, so stiff and pliable
at once, so crystalline and fluid. The peacock colors
changed from green to blue and back again as she
moved: the silk shifted tint somehow as feathers will. She
lifted her arms so the ample sleeves fell free, wide wings,
and then continued the motion to remove from her
coiled braids the bronze pins, skewers long enough to
reach a man's heart through his ribs. The rain outside,
the heat at her back, the silk on her skin immersed her in
nature, where there was no sin, no turning back. "Do I
look as you imagined?"

"A thousand times I believed I had imagined it, but I
had failed. There are realities we cannot conceive."

"Do I overfill it at my matronly age, so it hangs
less pleasingly than upon one of your bony Byzantine
whores?"

He did not answer the taunt; really the sight of her
seemed to have made Fengon stupid.

"Why are you standing so far away?"

He jumped a step, startled from his enchanted contemplation. "You commanded me to. You were severe with me."

"That was before you robed me in the costume of a Mediterranean jade. See, I have black hair. I have olive skin." Her face was hot; his stupefied gaze was a fire. His body, shorter and tenser than her husband's, radiated a rapt helplessness, his arms out from his body and curved as if carrying a great weight. "Come, my brother," she said. "What you robed, you may disrobe."

With those curving arms he lifted up the clinging tunic, and the chemise, its ties undone, came off with it. Geruthe pressed her rosy ripeness into the abrasions of Fengon's rough clothes. His riding shirt had leather shoulders to cushion mail. She inhaled the rain-drenched dead-animal smell. "Protect me," she whispered, adhering tight against him as if for concealment, her lips seeking the gap in his bristling wet beard.

Afterwards, she toyed with the long bronze pins, skewers for her hair, and held one to his naked chest as he lay beside her in the bed. With the point of the other she dimpled the white skin between her heavy breasts. "We could make an end now," she suggested, her eyes, widened and softened by love, sly with the possibility.

Fengon in his limp state considered her offer. Such a further and ultimate relaxation would conveniently crown his triumph. Gently he lifted the skewers from her grip, pinched the flesh beneath her chin, and weighed a warm breast in his palm. "I fear we have too much of our fathers in our natures," he said, "to give the world so easy a victory."

She felt this would happen but once, this unfolding of herself, and so she was luxuriously attentive to it, as if she were both storyteller and heroine, physician and invalid. In their hours of stolen intimacy, Fengon disclosed to her in the white mirror of his own body, furred and pronged, a self laid up within her inner crevices and for forty-seven years merely latent, asleep. All her unclean places came alive, and came clean. Did she not carry in her veins the warrior blood of Rodericke and of his father, Hother, the vanquisher of Guimon, who had betrayed Gevare and whose live body Hother burned in revenge? Protest had been lurking in her, and recklessness, and treachery, and these emerged in the sweat and contention of adulterous coupling.

She and Fengon seized what mattresses there were, at times too impatient for the convenience of the mock court they had established in Corambis's lodge: a grassy bramble not a league beyond Elsinore's moat, or a stone niche in a little-used gallery where hiked skirts and lowered breeches created sufficient access for their souls' emissaries, those lower parts so rich in angelic sensation. She would have lain down in warm mud for him, even the mud of the pigsty, to enter the exaltation she found in his brute love. He was not always gentle nor always rough; he maintained the small surprises of the seducer's art, which yet she had to feel arose involuntarily in him, to impart movement to the great element of herself beyond the control of her will.

Unlike Horvendile, Fengon was at home in the pit

of the flesh. His soul did not dart looks about for an exit to some safer, more public chamber, lit by social chatter and churchly candles. When done, the King was anxious to skulk off to his own closet; a nature-hating piety learned in Jutland unmanned him. Love's gratifications, violent and uncaring when part of his pirate raids, bordered in his mind on the Devil's domains. Whereas Fengon was content to loiter in a twinned concupiscence, telling Geruthe over and over, with his tongue and eyes and rethickened horn, all the truth about herself that she could hold. He uncovered in her not just the warrior but the slave. Had he bid her lie down in pigshit she would have squeezed her buttocks together in the clench and rejoiced to be thus befouled. At night, reliving the afternoon's embraces, she would lick her pillow in hunger to be with her lover again—her redeemer from lawful life's deadening emptiness, her own self turned inside out and given a man's bearish, boyish form. Her father's court had held no more eager slut than she.

Geruthe found she relished even the deception, the rank duplicity of having two men. Horvendile was pleased by how quickly he aroused her now. She tried to hold back caresses and tricks learned from his brother. Over the years her husband had turned to her ever more rarely, as little as once each waxing and waning of the moon, but now, roused by he knew not what disturbances below his horizon, he more often answered her body's silent call. Fengon sensed when she had been with her husband, though Geruthe would deny it. "You have the Hammer's smell," he accused. "You come to me already satisfied."

"Never satisfied but by you, Fengon. Only you know me. Only you know the way to my heart's heart, my inmost seat of passion. The other is but a duty, a duty of submission laid upon the wife by the stiff-mouthed priests, to whom we are sinful poor animals."

"But you *do* submit. Like the lowest trull, you spread your legs for a repulsive customer. I should beat you. I should pound the pale slime of that spouting cock from your gut."

"You may hurt me with words and looks," she warned, "but leave no marks."

His eyes flashed, reading her meaning. "So your dim and pompous husband, revelling in his liberties with you, may observe no traces of his maddened rival, no blue-black bruises left by a devil's hand."

His upper lip lifted in a snarl; she wanted to kiss him, for taking so serious a wound. Instead, she applied balm:

"He does not revel, Fengon. He exploits his rights, if he does, matter-of-factly, his purpose too blunt and damp to strike any spark." This was not quite the truth, not in her quickened duplicitous state; she felt the thrill of deception between her legs, where two men contended, one the world's anointed and the other her own anointed. She knew them, and neither wholly knew her. "Ardor is a matter of spirit," she continued in a reassuring vein, "more than of the body, for a woman. Many a wife perforce opens her arms to a man she hates."

"Do you hate him? Tell me you do."

Now that he begged her to lie, she could not. His doleful look was so earnest, she must try to be honest. "Near it, sometimes, but not quite. Horvendile's sins against me have been those of omission, whose pain is low and dull but unremitting. He saw me first as desirable property, and of his property he is a considerate enough caretaker. But, yes, in that he has taken from me the days of my life, and encouraged in me a mummifying royal propriety, I do hate him. You, by daring me to love, have led me to see how badly tended I have been. But the world is such. He is my master. Outside of Elsinore, I am nothing—less than a female serf, who has at least her native sturdiness, her hungry sprats, her beanpatch, her straw bed."

If Geruthe had hoped that Fengon would dispute her nothingness outside of Elsinore, she was disappointed. She felt the ratchet of desire in him slip, displaced by other, more thoughtful machinations. His brown eyes darkened—his black pupils expanded—looking into the future's cave. "What do we do," he asked, the grains in his soft voice each distinct, "if he discovers us?"

They were secluded in the round tower room of Corambis's lodge. They had removed their clothes and lay on the canopied bed as on a raft in a warm sea. A high-summer day flooded the air with the hum of insects and the humidity of growth pressing and snaking into every niche; the vine at the window sought to thrust its heart-shaped leaves inside. The trees all about and the surface of the lake glittered with a million shifting details, a sea of organic incidents in which the lovers' own incident drifted. But a cool shadow of forethought had fallen across their bodies; their rapture was chilled.

"How could we be discovered?" she asked.

"How could we be not, some day or other?" he asked. "The four around us know, and Corambis our absent host, and those at Elsinore who see you ride forth so faithfully, and those country folk who hail your passing, and the old couple who keep the cottage that guards our haven. All hold our truth hostage."

She closed her eyes. He was tipping her, sliding her off their raft, making her think toward their fathomless doom. "Why would any of them tell Horvendile?"

"Personal advantage, or interrogation under torture, or the innocent pleasure each soul takes in the mishaps of others. A righteous anger, perhaps, that the commandments which restrain the world's poor are disregarded by the mighty."

"I have been heedless," the Queen admitted, trying to consider herself. She sensed her body floating naked away from her thinking head—her breasts blown roses pink and white, her sex swollen and tender beneath its matted bush, her bare feet forming a distant audience of toes. "I was more indignant than I knew. Thirty years of lofty restriction gave intensity to my appetites and re-leased them without a proper thought of consequences. Or if there was a thought, it paled before a queen's hab-ituated belief in her entitlements. I was idly impulsive and selfish when you and I began, and now it would be death to let you go."

"Enamorata, it may be death to keep me," Fengon warned. "*Amor, mors.*" He stroked her tingling hair and tugged a strand in illustration. "Fate cuts the sailor some slack, but then the line pulls taut. The creditor allows some grace, but then the debt is pressed. We have been wallowing, these summer months, in the blithe interim. However, just as some are invisible by being small, our very size and nearness to the King may make us hard to see. His will to see is not keen, I believe, for once he does see he has an obligation to act. An obligation, if I know my brother, he will move circumspectly to discharge. The disruption to Denmark might dislodge him as well. The populace is not prudish in its sympathies. You are the throne to many, and I have my loyalists in Jutland and some well-placed friends abroad."

Her left hand returned from an idle investigation. "Ah, love, look—your little delegate to the lower parts has quite lost desire for your willing trull."

Fengon looked down to where his breeches had been removed. "Thoughts of being beheaded do have a retractive effect." He chucked her ruefully in the soft double plumpness beneath her chin. "I fear I am a fisherman who has lost his hook," he said, "and you will glide away, back to familiar waters."

"No, my lord, I am part of you now. We must glide on together." And indeed like a big fish she slithered down in the bed, to revive his manhood with a Byzantine technique he had taught her. She liked it, this blind suckling, this grubbing at nature's root. She fought gagging, and tugged at his balls. There was no need to think. Let be. His responsive needy swelling ousted every scruple from her head. Like maggots they would fatten, then fly.

"*Il tempo fa tardi*," Fengon said to Sandro upon at last emerging. "*Andiamo presto!*"

"Il giorno va bene per Lei?" The servant had sensed trouble coming.

"Sì, sì. Era un giorno perfetto. E per te?"

Herda, though sitting composed by the clean-swept cold fireplace, had a flushed, smoothed face, and there was something awry where her wimple was pinned to her chin band. Her lips looked rubbed, her eyes watery.

"Molto bene, grazie, signore. Crepi il lupo!" May the wolf burst!

That summer's warmth stretched into fall. October's days, golden with the turning of the beech and chestnut forests, had sun-warmed centers, though the dawns showed frost on the orchard grass and ice on the court-yard puddles. Each evening nipped some minutes from the day's length, and a crackling cold descended by midnight, revealing the first northern lights. They existed out of scale, in a star-strewn heaven cut to no measure but its own — waving tall curtains hung from nothing, disclosing nothing when they parted, unless it was dimmer folds of themselves, their evasive faint peacock colors, violet and turquoise, a far-off music of phosphorescence. They undulated along their vertical folds with a kind of beckoning motion, fading and returning.

The King was held to Elsinore more than in the summer, when he set forth for weeks at a time to survey his domains and call upon his provincial governors, themselves held in place by the need to supervise — or to keep watch upon those who did supervise — the burgeoning crops, the grazing herds, the game-ridden forests, the laborious harvests and the rightful taxes thereon, which the villeins and fiefholders tirelessly schemed to avoid. In their shortness of sight they did not comprehend that without the royal taxes there would be no royal armies and hired companies to defend them against the Norwegians and the Pomeranians and those many others who wished to conquer the land and make all Danes slaves. There would be no castles to give them shelter in an invasion, or bridges to carry them across rivers on the way to market and to the fairs and carnivals—carnivals where, it seemed to the King, men and women who should be working wasted days and health in gawking at freaks and frauds, in promiscuous mingling and in drunkenness and gluttony that made the clever stupid and the stupid stupider. The Church was short-sighted in multiplying saints and with them saints' days and excuses for fairs and folly. Soon there would be no workdays and purposes in common. Without a funded central authority, every hamlet would remain an island, and there would be no Crusades, or nobly sponsored tourneys, or unifying wars.

While King Horvendile was away ensuring that the land's riches provided the mite that was due the royal coffers, Geruthe and Fengon felt free to spend long hours together, sating not only their lust—which grew more rather than less, as practice and familiarity widened their liberties—but satisfying the innocent curiosity whereby those steeped in love feed upon the most trivial of the details that compose, particle by particle, the other's being. Fengon especially wished to possess her girlhood, to penetrate to the image of his full-fleshed mistress as a sturdy female child making her benign, broad-browed, solemn way through the confusions of Rodericke's court in the bereft years after her mother's death. He doted upon this little girl with her unblaming green-gray eyes and sweet small dark space between her front teeth—this rosy child in a brocaded cap that covered her ears and half of her cascading hair—a child neglected yet coddled, passed from the lap of one favorite lady to that of another and then impatiently returned to the care of her nurse, ancient gnarled Marlgar, who would take her to the high safe solar above the adult din, to her little sidewalled bed and rag dolls whose three names she still remembered after forty years, reciting them so fondly their clay-bead eyes and bunched noses and stitched smiles rose before her, as she told him all this, more than once.

"Were you lonely?" he asked.

"I think not," she answered, gravely thinking back, like looking for her reflection at the bottom of a well. "I had no brother or sister, but there were children my age in Elsinore, the children of inferiors. We played Saracens and knights, and dangled grasshoppers at the golden carp in the moat. Marlgar followed me everywhere but rarely denied me a game or a pleasure. She came from one of the small islands north of Lolland, where the children run free. My father could be gruff, and his friends in their drunkenness unseemly, but I knew I would come to no harm. I was a princess, I early knew, and wondered what prince I would love and marry; the thought of him was often with me. And now he is here, beside me."

"Oh, dear heart, I am not the perfect prince a child

imagines. I am a king's dark and disreputable shadow. Your little princess—she knew she would be always taken care of, without her willing it?"

"Yes. I could will little, but to be good and not complain."

"And you are like that still, passive and pleasant."

"I suppose so. Does it irk you?"

"It enchants me, and frightens me a little."

"Don't be frightened, my love. All that lives must die. To waste this life in fretful care for the next, or for a future calamity—that, too, is a sin. Birth lays upon us the natural commandment to love each day and what it brings."

"Geruthe," he exclaimed, taking pleasure as always in the rueful three syllables of her name, that spelled out her flesh in his mind. "Your wise sweetness, or sweet wisdom—how unreal our perils appear to you."

"No, they appear real enough, but then I made the decision to risk them. A woman as well as a man must keep her own accounts." She stroked his bare shoulders, smooth as armor but for a violet welt left by a Turkish scimitar. She trailed a fingertip down the scar, to where his bearish chest-hair began. "My agony in the travail of Hamblet's birth put life and royalty in my debt. I decided, it may be, at last to collect. My father and future husband together bargained me away, and you have given me back my essential value, the value of that little girl you so belatedly dote upon."

Fengon groaned. "Your trust sometimes crushes me. The world would say I have been base, as base as any squealing stoat who rushes where his lust points him."

She smiled. "You were discreet, and let all possible time go by. I was ready to receive you at my wedding. You sent an empty platter instead. As to the world, there is the truth from without, and the truth from within. The truth within is ours. I have found you trustworthy, and faithful to me. We cannot be destroyed, but by one letting the other go."

He kissed her hands, naked whenever she met him, though heavily ringed when she sat on the throne beside Horvendile.

In Elsinore, then, as winter approached through the golden days of harvest, the King could turn his attention to domestic matters. One fatal day, that day of bare slant light called All Saints', he summoned his brother to a private audience.

"Rumors reach me," the King began, "that you come to Elsinore more often than we meet, as brothers and comrades." He had taken on ballast since Fengon had last observed him, and held his head and torso as if the muscles of his thick neck ached.

"You have the kingdom to supervise, and I but my lagging estates, here and in our homeland. But for when the *råd* gathers, or the *thing* is called to convene, I would not obtrude my counsel."

"Your counsel and visible support mean much to the throne. After the Prince, none stands closer to it than you."

"But the Prince, from all accounts, is healthy, and, beyond his whimsical disposition, able."

"Able, but scandalously absent."

"Hamblet improves his mind in the realms of our

august ally the Emperor, to fit himself better to rule, when the time comes. But you are not old, and of our father's tough stock."

"Alas, not every noble Dane lives to die of decrepitude. Some are hurried along. I feel stiff and languid, often, but never mind. Who tells you the Prince is able?"

Fengon hesitated but a blink, before seeing no harm in an honest answer. "His mother and your Lord Chamberlain—both give a loving report of his manly abilities."

"Natural affection and politic courtesy shape their impressions. My son is a mystery to me."

"Though I have no claimed children, I believe it is ever thus, brother, with father and sons. The son's world differs from the father's if only by the dominating presence of the father in it. The same might be said of younger brothers and elder. You see clear to your objectives; I see always you ahead of me, intervening."

Horvendile's broad face, with its prim small mouth, sought briefly to encompass these geometries, sifting them for impudence. But he had some center of concern, and would not be dragged from it. "The Queen—you hold discourse with her frequently."

Alerted, Fengon became more deliberately urbane. He felt oddly weightless, all his senses on tiptoe. "My tales of exotic travel give some relief to her monotonous days. She has an adventurous mind, but is much pent-up in royal routine."

"This summer she went with me to Skåne."

"And enjoyed herself royally. She said you were admired and admirable."

"She talks much of me?"

"Of little else."

"And what is her tenor?"

"Dear old *frater*, you press me as if I were a partner in your marriage. She spoke adoringly, last spring on her return, of your exemplary goodness, your hard-won power, your love of your people, which they of course reciprocate."

"She thinks I am foolish, to love Denmark so possessively. She thinks I take too much to heart the old notion that if goodness does not flow from God through the King then the people will suffer and sink, all mutual obligations cancelled, and only an animal selfishness left, and savage anarchy. The King is the sun which warms the land. If something is amiss with him, his beams are bent. Crops fail, and rot infects the grain that is gathered and stored."

Images so grandiose tempted Fengon to raise a smile against them, saving his own sanity, fending off a vocabulary bloated by self-glorifying superstition. Kingship had driven Horvendile mad. The Hammer struck another blow: "I often wonder, brother, why you do not marry."

"Marry, I? Marriage seems to be the theme of this conference."

"We are not yet to the bottom of our themes. But bear with me, and ration your smiles. Lena of Orkney, whom you took to bride when my own wedding had shown the way, and whom I met and thought a suitable match for your dreaming, romantic nature, died untimely. You have been vital these decades since, traversing a continent of possible brides, and have shunned your clear duty to our family and to Denmark. You have not played your part in the enlargement of our interests. Even now, the daughter of the King of Scotland, ambassadors inform me, is sound and intelligent, and appetizingly young: a strong link between our courts would put the English in a tidy nutcracker."

Fengon did laugh, imprudently. "I would be happy to see the English in a nutcracker, but not one where my wife would form one handle, to be seized as you demanded. I wish no wife. I am beyond such wishing. I am an old soldier, accustomed to the friendly stench of men."

"You wish no wife. How can that be? Are you unnatural?"

"As natural as you, brother. More, indeed, since I have not made myself King by capturing an unwilling girl."

"Has Geruthe told you she was unwilling?"

"No, I surmised it. I surmised it at the time, and avoided witnessing your triumph, as brutal as your rape of Sela before you slew her."

"Sela was a scourge upon our coasts," Horvendile said calmly, his long eyes watchful. There was a fishy glaze to the whites of the King's eyes that belonged to the something amphibian about his lipless, decisive mouth. Fengon should not have let his anger out, defending a teenaged bride long gone from the earth, and who had perhaps been more willing than she admitted to her lover. His romanticism had betrayed him. When he had lunged to attack, the balance between the brothers had shifted.

"Perhaps you do not wish a wife," Horvendile said, heavily, dully, sure of his ground, "because you already have a wife of sorts—another man's wife. Don't speak, Fengon. Imagine this fable with me. A good and faithful king has a wandering brother, who comes to his castle at last, weary of fruitless adventuring, and in his embittered idleness seduces the Queen, with the aid of the King's treacherous, senile Lord Chamberlain. The adulterous couple sate their unspeakable lust month after month, in a secret shelter the pandering Lord Chamberlain has provided in his enmity to the King, whom he knows to be planning to relieve him of his lucrative post. I ask you, as my loving brother and trusted member of my *råd*, what should this so grievously abused king, the guardian of the Lord's commandments and protector of his own extended household, do?"

Fengon felt supernaturally quickened, his every nerve bathed in the soothing, cleansing liquor of emergency. The pit had opened under him, but it was no deeper than his own death, which must be borne in any case. As when in hand-to-hand battle with Turk or Saracen, Alsatian mercenary or Pisan, all facets of the situation flashed upon him at once, and the copiously tinted world was stripped to a few stark monochromes—the white of life, the red of blood and counterblow, the black of death. Fengon responded, "The King should first torture his sources for so bizarre and unlikely a tale, to persuade them to retract and confess their lies."

"My most informative source is not here to torture. He has gone back to Calabria. Our icy autumn nights frightened him with their portents of worse winter coming, and he betrayed you for safe passage to his sunny land of origin."

Fengon held silent, but he felt his flushed face speak for him. His years of diplomacy had overpersuaded him of his seductive powers, of a capacity to elicit loyalty, especially from young men and foreigners. The limits of language imposed a false closeness, a false bottom to his reading of another. He would have trusted Sandro with his life. He *had* trusted him with his life. *Crepi il lupo!*

Horvendile began to prowl the audience chamber, treading on pelts of wolf and bear, exulting in his mastery of the situation, demonstrating his vengeful ease. "Blame not just Sandro—many eyes observed, many tongues tattled. Even my own instincts, which I know you and Geruthe think are hopelessly dulled by my ponderous crown, told me something was amiss—or, rather, something had been added. She was different with me—more expressive, as if to make up in lesser confidences and gifts of attention the great secret she must withhold. She was, will it wound you to hear?, more ardent, rather than less as common decency might predict. She continued to simmer, removed from the fire. The fire of damnation, the priests would tell us—the priests who know the flesh by the book and by the lurid light of the confessional but not as we do, in nature, as a two-edged instrument, a forked violence and mending, the wellspring of nurture and the ruin of reason. Geruthe is decent," Horvendile went on, toying with them all, mere puppets in his mind. "She was not blithe about blackening my honor, which is coterminous with that of Denmark. Our marriage bed was still a shrine to her, though she defiled it. I benefited by her chagrin, without at first scenting the source. There was something, it would be too rude to say rotten, but overripe about her and her attentions."

He wants me to talk about her, Fengon realized. To describe her in terms as shameless as his own, as a forni-catrice abandoned to lechery, stewing in guilt, turning over and over, a plump morsel in a pungent sauce, deli-cious, her legs splayed to display her hairy hell-hole: only that way could Horvendile repossess her, through his brother, in those hours when she had stolen herself away. Glancing back through the dappled months of forbidden passion, Fengon remembered the watery play of light in their round chamber and out on the lake, and Geruthe's girlish voice flirting in delight at his gifts, and her mature rosy splendor pressed against him, as if to hide herself, at the moment of surrender. *Protect me*, she had begged.

Fengon still said nothing, just kept his gaze on his brother as the King prowled, in the lofty agitation of an inescapable predator. Horvendile saw that his brother would not share the naked spoils. He became irate. He sardonically accused, "You give me no counsel."

"I cannot be accused and judge both. Be aware, how-ever, that thrones can topple in convulsions they insti-gate. Under your reign as under any, Denmark is restless with perceived wrongs and conceivable gains. The men who profit under an established order are always out-numbered by those who have better hopes of a new."

"You dare read me instructions, you who have over-turned my household peace and my wedlock's dignity? Who won to your vile lust, stinking of foreign brothels, the will of my virtuous queen? You were always my inferior, Fengon—a filthy skulking shadow, less good at sport, less strong, less fair, less studious, the lesser favorite of our priestly tutors and our father, yes, I so assert though Gervendile sought to give us equal posts in Jutland, as if in battle we had done equal service, shown equal bravery and military wit."

Fengon, stung, touched the round-pommelled hilt, smoothed by much handling, of his sword. "I was less cruel than you," he said, "less the enraptured despoiler in Norway's helpless seaside parishes, but I deny that you had the edge of me in resourcefulness or courage."

Horvendile's long eyes had taken in his gesture. "You touch your sword? Would have at me? Come, brother, here is my breast, armored in velvet merely. You would not wound me worse than when you bewitched and pierced my most virtuous-seeming queen!"

His old trick of chest-baring, Fengon thought. *Archers may be hiding behind an arras. Or crouched in alcoves above, ready to make me a porpentine if I take a step toward his presence.*

"You were always foul at heart," the King was going on, in a reminiscent, loitering tone, as his brother's hand left the smooth hilt. "Your inevitable envy of me drove you to brooding, to unnatural introspection and fancy, in which you sought to embroil others, of the weaker, more suggestible sex. You idolized women and therefore sought to degrade them, knowing your exaltation to be unreal, the product of despicable cowardly fevers. Poor Lena, raised in those treeless island fields studded with ancient tombs, was a perfect match, with her own unreality, for your dominating fantastications. The blackest rumors have circled about her death, as to the abuses you imposed upon her innocence, but I have never believed them. I have believed you loved Lena as well as you could love any person not purely a figment of your blighted mind. Why have you hated me, Fengon? We shared the same parents, the same remorseless upbringing. I did not will my own excellence to spite you; you could have basked at my side with almost equal honor rather than infest the remote corners of Christendom with your perverse longings and expatriate's pride, wasting your life among heretics and sybarites."

Fengon said, "I do not hate you. I find you, for all that the world has conspired to puff you up, strangely negligible. And, as this interview proceeds, prating and tedious. What you think you know is less than the truth, but act upon it as you will. How do you answer your own question, concerning the hypothetical fable?"

"Death to the traitorous chamberlain, for a start," Horvendile stated.

"His white hairs and years of fealty would argue for mercy."

"They argue against it, enriching his affront. Evil long contemplated is evil doubled. A death by torture and quartering, as an example to other officials. The wicked brother—"

"Who has suppressed a thousand wicked thoughts—"

"—deserves obliteration but would be granted permanent exile. The execution of one whose same blood beats in the King might disrupt the plain minds of those who take us as divinity. Banishment is more grand than execution, suspending the sinner prolongedly in his regret and envy; it could even be construed a mercy, to one long self-exiled and one who would, like Satan, prefer retreat in the earth's bowels to having his eyes tormented by the radiance of his conqueror, his rightful lord."

"Fie, fie. And the Queen?"

Horvendile heard the tension in his brother's voice. He smiled: that lipless mouth so often pinched shut in cold-blooded snap judgment now broadened and prodded up his cheeks, twitching his skimpy beard's curls. "The Queen, you feckless infatuate, is the King's to dispose of. When our forefathers ruled in the mists, impaling was considered a fit punishment for offenses such as hers. Jörmunrekr, the bards relate, had Svanhildr pegged and trampled to death by wild horses, for her reputed adultery."

"She was falsely accused, and havoc was loosed, the legend goes on to report. Punish me, *burn* me, instead, or punish yourself. It was your neglect and contempt that Geruthe in her sweetness of womanly soul was seeking to repair."

"The Queen is mine, however grossly you have used her, and however you slander a marriage of which she exposed to you only the aspects that flattered you and excused her grotesque, incestuous adultery. Give her up, Fengon, along with all thought of your own good repute.

You both must be, for the sake of truth and order, disgraced. I will see your Jutland lands confiscated, and all connection to the royal rights disowned."

"Rights by inheritance more Geruthe's than yours," Fengon interposed.

Horvendile brushed the point aside. "You will wander as a pauper, Fengon, and the mark of shame and malice my hired tongues set upon you will make your murderer a hero. You will be less than dirt, for dirt has no name to dishonor. Burn, if you will burn, in the knowledge that beauteous Geruthe still sits wived to me, however chastened and grieved by such thorns of remorse in her bosom as will help her scarified soul to sing in Heaven, at the end of all our squalid trials."

His mind had moved on. Fengon felt himself in his brother's long icy eyes no more than a gnat to be crushed—already crushed, already a small smear on this page of history. Horvendile told him condescendingly, "The tortuous revenges of the past have no place in our Christian age; her fate is what it has been these thirty years, to be immutably my wife. You have misjudged me, my incestuous, covetous brother, if you think that I am second to you even in love of Geruthe. But my love is as firm and pure as yours has been wanton and rootless. Though base, you have no base; mine is as wide as Denmark. *Ha.*"

Horvendile had scored as neatly as when his broadsword severed King Koll's foot. Fengon felt blood impotently pour from him. To be severed from Geruthe . . . Her compliant good nature, after a time of grief and penitence, would entwine itself with her husband's again, and her weak flesh and gentle, sensible spirit yield back all that had been her lover's. He had been carved by this regal butcher to a core of defiance that as yet was without resource. Gutted of hopes, Fengon felt his soul pass from the mixed condition of common mankind to the adamancy of the Devil's party, blackened by a blind vow not to be overcome. He curtly bowed. "I await your judgment, then."

"Wait in silence a while. State business with ambassadors from Poland calls me this instant to a broader, more amenable sphere than that of this triple betrayal, which makes me heartsick, in truth. I take no joy in knowing that men are garbage, and women too, and that royal love and favor breed a voluptuous ingratitude."

"I beg you, pious brother, impale me if that would please you, but spare the obliging old man his head, and the Queen public disgrace, your private chastisements run as they will. She has ever taken an innocent pride in her status as Rodericke's cherished daughter."

"My announcements are of my sole determination, and any comment you deliver on the Queen is a knavish impertinence. I know her, too, remember. I vowed to cherish her. Speak not to me again. I curse you, brother, and the monstrous joke of nature that bade us issue from the same womb."

Thus ingloriously dismissed, Fengon was aware as he left the King's presence of the transformation working within him — cold distances opening up, beyond rage, through which his thought moved with the flashing speed of a duellist's reflexes. His romanticism had been boiled away. The bones of things were laid bare. Geruthe no longer loomed as the *princesse lointaine* or Form of Light but as a treasure he must seize back, a territory he must not lose. Still, he had no idea what he must do, only that he must stop at nothing. Like a tiercel aloft his mind glided, motionless, with black unhooded eyes, each patch of earth below magnified by its subdivision into many quickly perceived coverts, where life might lurk.

As he left the audience chamber, he saw the arras move near the doorway. He had not taken ten steps down the empty arcade outside the great hall before Corambis was beside him, breathing wheezily. The old man had heard it all and was terrified. His green sugarloaf hat had left his head, whose white hairs radiated from his bald spot as if fleeing in panic. Hectic red spots on his withered cheeks showed high excitement, yet his voice, that instrument of his life's work, had a revived timbre, a youthfully urgent diction restored by shock.

"He will be three hours at lunch," he said, as if a rapid conversation were being resumed. "The Polacks drink deep, and come to their sticking points the long way around. He will be heavy with wine. He will see no need to hasten in his dealings with us and the Queen, so fixed is his conviction of imperturbable power. He will, I wager, take his nap in the orchard as usual. It has become his fixed habit as the years bear upon him, in order to flee the claims of citizens and courtiers, to rest his watchful eyes and brain, an hour or possibly as much as two each afternoon in sleep, from April to October, and even into November, which All Saints' Day has just now ushered in, repelling the season's chill with furs, or thickly woven wool, or a close-knit cap upon his head, where in summer's heat no covering is needed—"

"Yes, yes. Get on. Less telling, and more told, Corambis. We can be seen and overheard here."

"—within a gazebo, or pergola, or some would say a belvedere or baldachino, built for this homely purpose of unshaved logs and boards but hastily planed, near the southern wall of the middle bailey, to catch warmth from the stones, there in the orchard, this side the moat and the other side, I say, of the bailey wall, in all but the least amenable of weathers, even in a rain not too windblown, so does His Majesty like the orchard air, in one season white with petals and loud with bees and in another heavy with green shade and now fragrant with fallen fruit and wasps that thrive on the deadfall—"

"*Tell* it, for God's sake."

"There he will sleep, alone, undefended."

"Ah, yes. And how is access?"

"A single set of spiral stairs, so tight two men could not pass, descends from the King's apartments to a narrow door to which few have the key, I being one, in case he ever needed to be summoned to a crisis of arms or of diplomacy."

"Give me it," Fengon said, and held out his hand for the little-used key, which Corambis fussily, tremblingly disengaged from a ring of others. Its rust stained Fengon's palm. "How many hours have I before he sleeps?"

"The gentlemen from Poland, as I say, are prone to divagate, prevaricate, and expostulate to a degree that makes prognostication—"

"Estimate. Our lives could hang on this."

"Upward of three hours, less than four. The day is warm for fall, he will not wait till the shadows have brought the evening chill."

"This gives me time to Lokisheim and back, if I ride like the very devil. I have a substance there whose chemistry is apt. He is always alone?"

"The moat defends him, and he luxuriates in being, for this interval, he who suffers constant observing, unobserved."

"I could make my way through the royal apartments, descend, and wait."

"My lord, suppose you are accosted?"

"I will say I seek the Queen. He from whom the secret needed to be kept now knows."

"Should I inform the Queen of what has just passed?"

"Tell her nothing. *Nothing.*" The old man winced as Fengon gripped his arm. "She must be kept innocent, for her sake and ours. Though she connived at love, she would balk at—at this necessary step. Only ignorance will keep her heart and countenance clear. The Polacks will hold him safe some hours, but do not, if you will keep watch, let her come into his presence, lest he may undelude her and give her a wound whose outcry exposes us all. Now tell me, is there any other way back into the castle from the orchard?"

Corambis tilted his dishevelled big head, a pumpkin

stuffed with the conspiracies of five decades of Danish rule. Even on the brink of his own quartering he relished a plot to which he was privy. He answered, "The drawbridge whereby the orchard pickers cross the moat will be up and chained for the winter. But"—a dim light dawned—"a hollow shaft descends from the hostlers' latrine in the stables. It might be scrambled into and thence up. But for a gentleman, the filth—"

"I'll judge that nicety. Let us part smartly, and hope to meet again. If not in this world, in the interminable next."

Fengon had become an unfeeling tool in his own furious grip. By himself he saddled his horse, luckily his fastest, the black Arabian, now going gray in the muzzle. He fumbled at the buckles, cursing Sandro, who used to handle the Genoan saddle with such loving deftness. Mounted at last, and waved out through the barbican gate, he galloped the twelve leagues to Lokisheim, through the Forest of Gurre and beyond, driving his horse to a lather like that within his heated clothes. His retainers received him with amazement, since he had left but at that dawn, and blanketed and watered the shivering steed while Fengon rushed inside.

What he sought lay hidden in the carved rope-handled coffer beneath the crossed halberts. When he undid the fish-shaped clasps and lifted the lid, out flew the iodine scent of the Aegean. Toward the bottom, beneath layers of folded silks and worked leather and carvings of ivory and cedar—reserve treasures had his wooing of Geruthe needed them—he found a thick jade cross, Greek in that its arms were of equal length. A lady had once given it to him. "In case you meet an enemy," she had languidly explained. Younger then, thinking to strike a courtly tone, he had said something stupid about fearing no enemy if she remained his friend. She was older than he, and had waved away the flattery. In Byzantium, it was understood that lives and loves simply end. She had said, "Just as the cross holds both the agony of death and the promise of eternal life, so the juice of hebona combines the essences of yew and henbane, with other ingredients inimical to the blood's humors. Introduced into the mouth or ear, it produces an instant curdling, a violent brother to creeping leprosy. Death is quick, though terrible to behold, and certain."

Sealed by crimson wax, one of the cross's two equal arms had been laboriously hollowed to conceal a stoppered slender vial of Venetian glass. Fengon dug away the wax with the point of his bodkin and the vial slipped out. The lethal liquid had precipitated a fine brown sediment in its years of concealment; lightly shaken, it cleared to a pale yellow, which even here in the dark low hall caught a glow from somewhere. Suppose she had lied? She had lied often otherwise. She had lied idly, for the joy of creating multiple worlds. Fengon's hands shook, jarred by his ragged breathing, as he lifted the liquid to the light, then slipped the little vial into the inner pocket of his doublet. His rump and the insides of his thighs were sore; the small of his back screamed with his ride's repeated percussion. He was old, old; he had squandered his life. He smelled to himself of old age, of wet straw gone fusty, unforked in the stable.

The gallop back to Elsinore was urged to the edge

of the Arabian's capacity. Fengon whipped the aging horse mercilessly, while vowing aloud, yelling crazily in the animal's uncomprehending ear—its hairy exterior perked, its interior lilylike and a tint akin to human flesh—to put him out, if his heart did not burst, to lush pasture with a herd of plump mares. Answering the watchman's shout in full stride, Fengon thundered across the moat, beneath the spiked portcullis, into the barbican and the outer bailey, which on one side accommodated the stables. No hostler was on hand: good. One less witness, if witnesses were ever sought. He stalled the horse himself. He patted the soaked black nose, the blood-spattered nostrils, and whispered to the beast, "May I do as bravely." Two rides of two hours each had been achieved in scarce three. Fengon's image was squat and miniature, a bearded troll, in the long-lashed orb of the horse's eye, with its purple iris.

Feeling airy and shaken again on foot, he glided unchallenged along the inner wall to the lesser hall, up wide stairs troughed with centuries of wear and through the deserted lobby to the great hall, up stairs again, more stealthily, through the audience chamber and into the King and Queen's own fir-floored suite. He heard from several rooms away a lute and the thready entwined voices of recorders—the Queen and her ladies were being entertained, while they stitched at their embroidery frames. Perhaps the King's footmen had gone to listen. With a snake's silence Fengon moved through his brother's deserted solar and found the opening, low like the niche that holds a church's basin of holy water, which led to a spiral stair. It rubbed him on all sides, so narrow it was, and lit but by one *meurtrière* halfway down. The vertical slot of landscape—flashing moat, part of a thatched house, smoke from something being burned in a field—made his eyes wince and set a watery light on the curved wall behind him.

He descended into a well of darkness. The dry planks and rusted iron strapwork of a door met his fingertips; he stroked these mixed rough surfaces for the keyhole, as one strokes a woman's body for its secret small site of release. He found it. Corambis's key fit. The oiled works turned. The orchard outside appeared to be empty. He had arrived first. Thank—who? Not the Devil, Fengon didn't want to believe he was forever in thrall to the Devil.

Warming sunlight struck gold from the unscythed grass. Rotting apples and pears filled the air with a scent of fermentation. His boots crushed fruit, pulpy and fallen, and left telltale impressions in the tangled hay. His pounding heart kept company with the cold, abstract resolve of his will. There was no other course, improvised and chancy though this one had had to be.

He heard footsteps above, within the wall—such closeness of timing showed the hand of Heaven. He crouched behind a wagon used previously to hold the orchard's harvest of a month ago and now abandoned, with careless peasant husbandry, to the winter weather coming. He fingered the thick cross bulking in his doublet. The jade edges had been filed and the surfaces ground to the smoothness of skin and then incised in circular patterns like lace to the touch. He tried to think of fair and rosy Geruthe but his soul was narrowly, darkly intent upon the hunt, the kill.

The King emerged from the arched opening at the base of the bailey wall. His royal robes were brilliant in the low slant of sunshine. His face looked bloated and weary, naked in its ignorance of being observed. Fengon now slipped the vial from its socket and with a thumbnail worked at the stopper, a bead of glass held in place by a glue aged to the hardness of stone. Perhaps it would not come off; perhaps he must slink away, the deed undone. But away to what? Ruin, and not only for him—for one who had asked, *Protect me*. The bead of glass worked loose. Its film of liquid stung his forefinger.

From behind the abandoned, weathering wagon Fengon watched his brother shed a blue velvet robe and drape it over the foot of the pillowed couch set, as on a small roofed stage, upon the gazebo's raised floor. The King's surcoat was a golden yellow, his tunic snow-white linen. The cushions on his couch were green; he set his eight-sided jewelled crown on a pillow near his head and tugged up a blanket of dirty-gray sheepskin. He lay staring skyward while his folded hands fiddled upon his chest, as if revolving within himself the information that he had been cuckolded and must wreak a thorough vengeance on the criminals. Or perhaps the parley with the Polacks had gone disturbingly. Fengon feared the agitated monarch might not sleep at all, and pondered the possibility of rushing forward and compelling Horvendile to drink the contents of the vial, hurling the poison down his howling red throat like molten lead into the mouth of a heretic.

But suppose the assault fell short, and the King's

shouts brought help? Then a traitor's cautionary public mangling would be Fengon's fate. In Burgundy he had seen a staked plotter compelled to watch dogs gobble his unravelled intestines, there on the ground before him; the loyal crowd had thought this an excellent patriotic entertainment. In Toulouse he had been told of Cathars burned in bundles like fagots, only they burned more reluctantly, feet and ankles charring first. He understood from men who had survived torture that the spirit achieves another level, from which it looks down upon the body and its tormenters serenely, as from the lip of Heaven. In such a hovering mood he now waited, and when the sparrows and titmice above his head and about him in the twigs had ceased to mark his presence with twitters and scoldings such as would warn of a cat, he stepped forward to test if his brother's long blue eyes were still open. Had they been, he would have pretended to have come to plead, and looked for an opportunity to force the poison.

But from the King's belvedere issued, louder than the hum of wasps in the sugared grass, the rumble of snoring, of oblivious breathing. Fengon drew near, one tread at a time through the lank dying grass, with the unstoppered vial.

His brother slept in a familiar position, curled on his side, loose fist tucked against his chin, as Fengon had often observed when they shared a bed and then a doubly bedded chamber in lonely Jutland, where the winds made sleep fitful. Fengon had been, though younger, the lighter sleeper. Horvendile had daily exhausted himself in pushing ahead, in acting the elder and seizing his prerogatives in games and jousts, in exploration of the heath and the barren hilltops around them. Gervendile, bent upon raiding and carousing in imitation of the pagan gods, and with a wife who had withered to torpor in Jutie's ceaseless wind, let his sons run to nature. In their abandonment Horvendile did parental service, commanding but leading, rebuking but bringing his slighter, less prepossessing brother along with him, across the lag of eighteen months between their births. Across the heather, through the thickets, in pursuit of game with slingshot and longbow, sharing the sharp air, the hurrying wide sky. Had there not been love in this, from both sides? Alas, love is so pervasive, so ready to arise from our childish helplessness, that it would freeze all action, even that act needed to save a man's life and make his fortune.

As of their own volition Fengon's boots had silently slithered up the two steps to the platform where the King slept on his side, one ear up, his face slack. To pour the vial Fengon had to lift a lock of his brother's fair hair, still soft and curled low on his head, where not yet thinned by age and the pressure of the crown. His was a tidy ear, square and white and plumply lobed, with a froth of gray hairs around the waxy hole. Fengon's sucked breath caught in his teeth as he poured. His hand did not tremble. His brother's ear-hole, the hole that had taken in Sandro's poisonous words, a whirlpool that led to the brain and to the universe the brain constructs, accepted the pale juice of hebona with some, at the last,

overflowing; Horvendile in his sleep brushed clumsily at
the spot, as if at a wasp tickling at a dream. Fengon
stepped back, clutching the emptied vial in his fist. Who
was the Hammer now? His pounding blood made his
muscles jump.

He did not dare reënter the spiral stair, so constricted
and entrapping. At its head he might meet footmen, or
the Queen with her ladies and musicians. Crouched
low, he scuttled along the crooked bailey wall to where,
as devious Corambis had promised, a stone chute emptied toward the moat but could be attained on the pro-
tuberances and chinks of the masonry and—Fengon
gritting his teeth, holding his breath against the smell—
mounted by pressing arms and legs outward and climbing. There was no ivy as when he had first scrambled up
to Geruthe, but years of piss had eroded the mortar to
create footholds; slime coated rocks in whose sunless
crannies great white centipedes bred, daily supplied with
noxious nutrient. The bright gap toward which Fengon
squirmed upward was narrow but not narrower than
Geruthe's lancet window. He had wriggled through that
and now this, like fatty smoke rising in a flue, like excre-
ment reversing its course, sweating and grunting and
begging God or the Devil that no hostler or guard be
presently called by nature to this privy. If he were, Fengon's dagger would have to come into play, one murder
demanding another.

But his emergence from the garderobe was unobserved. He brushed at the noxious dampness on his tunic
and breeches and flitted along the bailey and barbican

walls to where his black Arabian still panted. He stood
next to the horse, to merge his odor with its sweat. He
shouted for a groom, to make a witness that he had
freshly arrived at Elsinore. The vial and jade cross he
dropped at first opportunity into the moat. Though at
his later leisure he was plagued by remorse and fear of
God's creeping justice, Fengon felt no holy qualm just
yet, in the fresh relief of his feat; his religion had
become cold necessity, and his form of worship lucky
acrobatics upon the bare bones of things.

The corpse was not found until another hour had
passed and the unknowing Queen sent a man down to
wake her husband. Horvendile's body, frozen with un-
seeing eyes bloodied and bulged outward, lay covered
with a silvery crust, leperlike, all his smooth skin turned
loathsome, all his body's liquids curdled. Fengon and
Corambis, taking charge in the confusion, gave out the
speculation that a venomous serpent nested in the
unmown orchard grass had sunk its fangs into the fair
and noble sleeper. Or else a distemper of the blood, long
festering unseen, had abruptly broken out; the King had
appeared joyless and brooding of late. At any event, amid
this calamity the kingdom, its foreign enemies astir, must
be administered, and the stricken queen comforted.
Who better than the brother of the King, whose only
son the Prince had been for over a decade immured in
futile studies at Wittenberg?

III

THE KING was irate. "I com*mand* that he come back to Denmark!" Claudius announced to Gertrude. "His insolent self-exile mocks our court and undermines our fledgling rule. He stays away to do just that. Though we have named him the next to take the throne, our own seat thereupon having been, in part, compelled by his prolonged withdrawal from Denmark, and urged upon me by my colleagues on the *råd* and ratified by the *thing*, swiftly convened in Viborg—for all of this, he sulks in absentia and, when he does deign appear, seems skittish to the point of madness. So belatedly did he attend his father's funeral, and so readily leave once the great bones were interred, that his friend Horatio—a *capi*tal fellow, I've asked him to stay as long as he desires, and to give the crown his counsel at his pleasure—Horatio never had the chance to greet him!

His best friend was ignored, and the populace could take no impression of an apparition so fleeting. Hamlet plays the ghost, a presence spun of rumor, to spite me, for the people have ever had him in their favor, and his absence at Elsinore purposely saps our reign of credibility!"

Gertrude was not yet accustomed to hearing her lover speak like this, at such length, with such pomp. Even in their privacy now he spoke as if there were others about them, courtiers and emissaries, the human furniture of rule. Two weeks had passed since her husband had perished in the orchard, unattended, unshriven, like some nameless pauper who eked his living on a Baltic beach, or like some soulless little rag of a woodland prey snatched up in sharp talons. Already Fengon, to her eye, had become bulkier, more majestic. He had named himself Claudius at the coronation, and Corambis, following his master into the imperial dignity of Latin, had taken the name of Polonius. "I think he means no harm to you or to Denmark," she began, half-heartedly defending her son.

"Denmark and I, my dear, are now synonymous."

"Of course—I think it's wonderful! But as to little Hamlet, there have been so many sudden changes, and he really did adore his father, though they weren't much alike, in subtlety or education. The boy needs time, and he feels at ease in Wittenberg, has companions there, and his professors—"

"Professors professing seditious doctrines—humanism, usury, market values, the monarchy as something less than the pure gift of God—the boy is thirty, it's time he came home to reality. Do you *really*," he went on, in a tyrannical accusatory vein that reminded her sadly of his

predecessor on the throne, "think he *is* in Wittenberg?
We have no idea if he is or not. 'Wittenberg' is just his
word for 'elsewhere'—elsewhere than Elsinore!"

Gertrude blurted, "It's not you he's avoiding. It's me."

"You, his own mother? Why?"

"He hates me, for wishing his father dead."

The King blinked. "Did you?"

Her voice was thickening; the habit of tears had been
reëstablished in her eyes these two weeks, and now she
felt them warmly gathering once more. "My grief wasn't
enough to suit him. I didn't want to die myself—to
throw myself on his father's pyre, so to speak, though of
course they don't have pyres any more, that was barbaric,
these poor drugged slave girls. . . . And I couldn't stop
myself from thinking that now there was no chance of
Hamlet's, my husband Hamlet's, finding out about *us*.
I dreaded that, though I pretended not to, I didn't
want to worry *you*. I was re*lieved*. I hate myself, admit-
ting it. Even dead, Hamlet has a way of making me feel
guilty, for being less good and public-spirited than
he was."

"Yes, well. I lived with that all my life—you just married into it."

"Now little Hamlet has it, that same gift. Of making
me feel dirty and ashamed and unworthy. I have a confession. No, it's too terrible to say." She waited to be
coaxed, then went on, uncoaxed. "All right, I'll *tell* you:
I'm *glad* the child isn't at Elsinore. He would sulk. He
would try to make me feel shallow, and stupid, and
wicked."

"But how would he know . . . anything?"

How like a man, Gertrude thought. *They want you to do everything to them, but then are too fastidious to name it. Claudius just wants things all to go smoothly, now that he is king, the past sealed off, history. But history isn't dead like that; it lives in us, it got us here.* "Children just *know,*" she said. "We're all they have to study at first; they become experts. He senses everything; I've terribly disappointed him. He wanted me to *die,* to be the perfect stone statue of a widow, guarding the shrine of his father for him forever, because it has his childhood sealed up in it also. Adoring his father for him is a kind of self-adoration. They were two of a kind—too good for this world. The night we were married, Hamlet didn't even look at me naked. He was too drunk. You, bless you, *looked.*"

His wolfish teeth showed a smile in the dark fleece of his beard, a flash of white like the white spot in his hair. "No man could have helped looking, my love. You were, are, sublime in every part."

"I'm a fat spoiled forty-eight-year-old, but being called sublime feels somehow *right.* As a kind of *play.* Hamlet—big Hamlet—didn't know how to *play.*"

"He played only to win."

Gertrude suppressed the observation that Claudius, too, in his new majesty, showed an inclination to win. But, then, having spent her life in the company of kings, Gertrude knew that for a king losing usually meant losing your life. High position entailed a precipitous fall.

"I'm fond of him, actually," Claudius said. "Young Hamlet. I think I can give him something he never had from his own father—he and I are fellow victims of that obtuse bruiser—that Koll-killer. We're alike, your son and I. His subtlety, which you mentioned, is much like my own. We both have a shadow-side, and a yen to travel, to get away from this foggy hinterland, where the sheep look like rocks and the rocks look like sheep. He wants *more*, to learn more."

"I thought you said he doesn't really go to Wittenberg."

"He goes *some*where, and learns *some*thing, that gives him dissatisfaction. I tell you I *feel* for him. We're both victims of Danish small-mindedness—Viking blood-hunger crammed into the outward forms of Christianity, which no one up here has ever understood, from Harald Bluetooth on; for him it was just a way to preëmpt a German invasion. Christianity turns grim in lands of frost; it is a Mediterranean cult, a religion of the grape. Truly, I am certain I can make the Prince love me. I appointed him my successor on my own impulse."

"He may resent that he remains a prince, while you occupy his father's throne."

"How could he resent that? He was never *here*, he showed no interest in learning the art of rule—of all that threatens and upholds a government. Some whisper," Claudius told Gertrude with lowered voice and subdued expression, "that he is mad."

She shivered. "He is sane, and shrewd," she said, "but still I cannot grieve on his absence. If he comes home, I sense that he will bring unhappiness."

"But come he must, lest a rebel faction form outside Elsinore's walls, and here is the scheme to bring him: marry me."

Her impulse was to greet his words with joy; but these

disrupted times shaded their import somberly, and like little weights they took her heart lower. "My husband, your brother, is but two weeks dead."

"Another two, and it will be a month—lag enough for such seasoned meat as we. Gertrude, don't deny me the natural outcome of my long and perilous devotion. Our present situation, scattered awkwardly through Elsinore's royal apartments, is too curious; we must sneak and tryst as if your husband's ghost keeps jealous guard over your virtue. Our union will settle all jangling gossip and give Elsinore a solid base—a master and a mistress." *And cement my hold on the throne*, Claudius did not say.

"I doubt it will settle Hamlet," said the Queen. The name's persistent doubleness—father, son; king, prince—brought a lump to her throat, as if it were too large to swallow.

"I wager the contrary," said Claudius, bluff and headlong in his decisions as kings must be. "It will restore his mother to the highest status, and supply an uncle in place of a father. Our wedded example will strengthen and steady his courtship of Ophelia, which you and Polonius both desire—you for the sake of your son's health and sanity, he to gain his daughter high estate. I do not begrudge the old man that boon of perpetuation; he served our own wooing well."

His speaking brusquely of their "wooing" touched a sensitive area in Gertrude. Though she had been bold and brazen enough in placing herself at a lover's disposal while still wedded to the King, when the ruthless irregularity of her behavior could be lightly scanned by her conscience as the enactment of a romance such as had

beguiled her betranced days of married boredom, her es-
capade took on a live soreness since the King's death: she
felt her fall had somehow caused the adder in the orchard
to sting the sleeping cuckold. At the same time, Sandro
had disappeared, and she wondered if there was a reason
she didn't know. Claudius, questioned, had said the boy
had become homesick with winter's onset, so he had let
him go south, with a tolerant bonus. It was strange this
had been done so suddenly, without her knowing.
Claudius in his old guise had spoken to her with the careless freedom of one with nothing to hide; now there was
a certain formality, a pregnant circumspection. Yes, it
would be good to bundle and hide the whole affair—the
lakeside lodge, the small troop enlisted in their deceit,
the hectic gratification of belonging to two men at once,
the pagan shamelessness—within the unimpeachable,
unbreakable contract of a royal marriage. Blushing as if
once again garlanded in virginity, Gertrude consented.

Claudius clapped his hands: a politic and lucrative
bargain had been struck. The date was set. Messengers—
to Wittenberg, to Laertes in Paris, to the capitals of
friendly powers—were sent posting on their way. Even
with so muted a celebration in prospect, a marriage
draped in mourning, Gertrude found these narrowing
November days brightened. What we once did imper-
fectly, we yearn to perfect in the second doing.

The guests were far fewer than when good King Roderick had assembled the flower of the Danish aristocracy
along with officials from the farthest reaches of Danish

power in Sweathland and nether Slesvig. Colored wimples and diamond-patterned doublets had become fashionable, and asymmetrically colored hose, even on the old and staid. Heavy necklaces and chains of hammered gold were consigned to the garb of mayors and officials, and the bells Gertrude had worn about her waist when she was seventeen would be considered now a quaint relic. And either she drank less wine and mead than on that giddy, frightening, flattering first occasion, or her capacity for alcohol had improved. The words of the service, which she had been too excited to listen to the first time, this time struck her with their touching archaism, their talk of plighting troth and of no man putting asunder—"asunder" a word employed on no other occasion. *Until death us do part.* Gertrude wondered how soon that would be. How could it be at all? Yet an eternal parting had occurred, at a stroke, on the mild afternoon of All Saints' Day, a serpent in the sunny orchard grass.

She and Claudius had debated the matter of music and dancing. Perhaps there should have been none, within a month of King Hamlet's death. And yet life must go on, and some of the guests had travelled from as far as Holsten, Blekinge, and Rügen. Subdued music, the espoused agreed—a lute and a recorder trio, with a timbrel to keep the beat—might form a background, like a faded tapestry, to the midday feast, and if dancing was generated afterwards, let it occur. She and the King, to establish the propriety of a reserved celebration, led a few measures of the *ductia*, its slow gliding movements almost like a dirge, she thought, her vision hazed by the

smoke of the rushlights and the fires roaring in the great
hall's two barrel-vaulted fireplaces. Her weddings took
place in winter, she thought, but to the verge of this
December the snows had been but dustings. Heaven
has been withholding. Claudius as he glided beside her,
taking her hand and releasing it to turn and take the
other, felt somehow removed by his having become her
husband. His touch was rigid and tense with his new
responsibilities. She had loved, when they had met dangerously in Gurre Forest, his relaxation into lawlessness,
his abandon to the moment once he had achieved his
goal—conquest of her, regardless of the consequences.
Now they were living into an aftermath of consequences,
treading in time to the timbrel, trying to survive the ex-
tinction of the adulterous, rapturous couple who had
existed outside Elsinore's walls. The seducer had become
a public man, his far-off beloved a daily presence.

He let go her hand when the music paused, and left
her to greet their guests, the high subjects of his reign.
She watched him—the fur collar of his robe upright and
its rim glittering as if with frost, the gold cross on his
chest reflecting red flashes of firelight—move to Hamlet
and Laertes, who had been talking together, bonded by
their knowledge of the world south of Denmark. Laertes
sported a dark goatee shaped like his father's white one,
and Hamlet had grown a red beard. A delicate beard, less
curly than his blond father's: its redness was a version of
the pale coppery tint of her own luxuriant head, and of
her tufts elsewhere. The gauzy beard repelled her; it
seemed an intimate aspect of herself lodged within him,

which he had decided to flaunt. He was daring her, in the fullness of his thirty years, to assert maternal control over his face. She could no more do that than consciously control her disposal of herself in love and marriage. Always between them, mother and son, stood her failure to feel herself loved enough by his father—a transparent, unsayable obstruction through which he gazed at her as if through the caul in which he had been born. He had hurt her so much, being born. No person had ever hurt her as Hamlet had, while the Battle of Thy was being won.

She could see, from the twists of his beautiful, ruddy, almost feminine lips, that Claudius was speaking French to Laertes and German to Hamlet, establishing himself with them as another man of the greater world, though his languages might be rusty, not as supple and freshly acquired as theirs. She worried that Claudius, his cosmopolitanism already faintly dated, would be mocked; but both younger men responded, as best she could make out, courteously, in Laertes' case with some animation, in Hamlet's with an expression masked by that disturbing beard, still so sparse the pallor of his cheeks glanced through. She trembled in fear for her husband, drawing dangerously close to her son. Her son was his enemy, she could feel in her loins. Claudius's hopes for winning the boy over seemed deluded folly to her, but, then, his courting of her, his impossible romantic love, had been carried through to this triumphant nuptial conclusion. To her relief, Claudius moved on, he had to greet everyone; he was the star, the center of the occasion, he had to parcel himself out equally. Gertrude knew how that was, having been since birth a star herself, a king's only progeny, the focus of envious and possessive eyes while still in her cradle.

Polonius, twinkling in a flowing new houppelande, came up to her and, having noted the direction of her gaze, said, "Our king bears himself well, as one long accustomed to preëminence."

"I confess I did not know," she said, "he would measure up so willingly. I thought he was a wanderer, a well-born vagabond."

"Some men, Your Majesty, wander in order to return with sufficient strength to achieve their long-nursed goals."

Gertrude did not like to think that Claudius had, like his brother, sought the throne. She preferred to think it had fallen to him by unhappy accident. True, he had shown initiative and singleness of purpose in seeking endorsement from the *råd* and election from the four provincial *thing*, and had by swift letter elicited allegiance from the bishops of Roskilde, Lund, and Ribe; but she ascribed all this to the good cause of stifling chaos in the wake of calamity. In those stunned days after Hamlet was found dead, and not only dead but hideously transfigured, like a long-buried statue disintegrating in shining flakes, Gertrude had been directing her attention elsewhere, inward, to her ancient task of mourning, of shouldering bereavement. For almost the first time in her life since the onset of menses she had felt transformed by illness, unable to leave the bed, as if her proper place were beside Hamlet in his clay grave, in the loathsome burial ground outside the walls of Elsinore, where mist clung to the tufted soil and the shovels of chattering gravediggers were always pecking away at the underworld of bone. Thus isolated, visited only by Herda, who had her own reasons for grief, for Sandro was gone and her belly was swollen, and by her whispering ladies-in-waiting, whose faces were rapt with the thrill of the recent horrific event, and the castle physician, with his dropsical bagcap and bucket of writhing leeches, Gertrude played doctor to her own spiritual symptoms, wondering why her grief felt shallow and tainted by relief. The King's weight had been rolled off her. He had never seen her as she was, fitting her instead into a hasty preconception, his queen. It did occur to her, later, that in this interval some other queen might have been forwarding her son's claim to the throne. But Hamlet had attended his father's burial and disappeared again. Her maternal instinct told her that the throne of Denmark with all its petty, bloody taxes on the soul was an acquisition he would snub. Nor had Polonius in his renewed dignities advanced the Prince's cause: there smoldered an animosity between them, a dislike passed from father to son. It was all, while she sickly dozed, and listened to her female visitors' own complaints, too entangled for her, like a basket of embroidery thread a kitten has slept in. When she stirred again, a presentable widow, all had been settled elsewhere in Elsinore and King Claudius approached her begging for her hand. She could hardly deny him; he had adored her from afar and, come closer to flesh out his fantastic image of her, had proven entertaining and responsive to the realities of her person. She would train him out of his overestimation gently, day by day, keeping alive the cherished little princess he had revived. It was too soon to marry him, perhaps, yet what else was she to do? Bereaved queens sometimes entered nunneries, but nuns seemed unhappy women to her—married to a preoccupied God and as sallow and shrewish as sublunary neglected wives. She liked the luxuriant, silky-stiff texture of Claudius's beard, the nutty scent of his bare chest. She liked his vagrant, insolent energy, now harnessed to the performances of kingship.

This wedding night was very different from her first. Then the groom could not stay awake, now he could not rest, though the celebration, relatively muted, had subsided in a flurry of polite departures, and the midnight bells had, like a crowd dispersed but returning to search for a lost glove or purse, reappeared as a lonely single clang, and then two. He had made love to her triumphantly, his nutty smell becoming mixed with an odor like the brackish scent close to the shore of the gray-green Sund. Surges of sensation in her lower parts lifted her so high her voice was flung from her like a bird's lost call; yet still, their wedded desires so gratified, he could not sleep. In the heated space of their curtained bed she could not drop off, feeling his male sinews still taut in him. Each time her thoughts had begun to dissolve into rumpled nonsense—reality's patterns folded chimerically—an abrupt motion of his beside her tugged her back into the clear night.

"Sleep, husband," she said softly.

"The day will not let go. Old Rosencrantz was telling me that young Fortinbras must be crushed and the Norwegian threat put to rest for good. These venerable nobles still live in a dream of heroic violence, of crushing and burning and final solutions. At the same time they grow fat on their share of the commerce that international peace brings."

"Hamlet used to say just that." She had spoken too quickly in her drowsiness, uttering a poisoned name. Her betrayed husband, his envied brother. She hurried on: "Polonius thinks you're a marvellous king already."

"He has personal reasons to believe and hope so. His good opinion has been already bought."

By what? Gertrude sleepily wondered. "He told me—a group of us, actually, gathered around—that you'll take us back to the days of King Canute. Not the saint, the original one."

"The one who couldn't stop the tide from coming in."

There was a dark sardonic undertow to his tone that tugged her awry. However bright the wedding torches, you marry a man's shadow side, too. She explained, "The one who conquered all England and Norway."

"And who, if I recall my history, made a pilgrimage to Rome to repent his many sins."

"Is that what you want to do?" she asked shyly. The idea of such a harsh pilgrimage seemed remote, cozy as she was. In bed with Claudius she felt as she had when a girl, on a freezing winter night, laid in her cot in a tumble of furs, that tingled and tickled and were tucked tight around her, so her body revelled in a warmth stolen from these other creatures. Marlgar, huddled in a hooded cloak, would sit a while silently with her, and the stars through her paneless window would shine as bright as icicle tips glinting in the morning sun. She wondered if, the way they had begun in sin, her husband saw her as tainted. The brothers shared this somber Jutland religious streak, that refused to accept the world at face value, as a pure miracle daily renewed.

"Not yet," Claudius said. "Not until Denmark is in perfect order. And I will take you with me, to see holy Rome and those other sun-soaked congeries beyond the Alps."

He turned his back, and seemed minded at last to sleep, now that he had stirred her up. She resented it. He was making her into Marlgar, awake while he drifted off. She said, "I saw you talking to Hamlet."

"Yes. He was amiable enough. My rusty phrases of German amused him. I don't understand why you are afraid of him."

"I do not think you can charm him."

"Why not, my love?"

"He is too charmed by himself. He has no need for you or me."

"This is your own son you are speaking of."

"I am his mother, yes. I know him. He is cold. You are not, Claudius. You are warm, like me. You crave action. You want to live, to seize the day. To my son, everything is mockery, a show. He is the only man in his universe. If there are other people with feelings, then that just makes the show more lively, he might concede. Even I, who love him as a mother cannot help doing, from that moment when they place the cause of your pain in your arms, this newborn wailing and whimpering in memory of your joint ordeal—even me he views disdainfully, as evidence of his natural origins, and proof that his father succumbed to concupiscence."

Claudius's voice became sharp: "Yet in my dispassionate estimation he appears witty, large-minded and many-sided, remarkably alert to everything around him, engaging to those worthy of being engaged, excellently educated in all a gentleman's arts, and handsome, most women would surely agree, though the new beard makes perhaps a hostile impression, concealing more than it enhances."

Gertrude said gropingly, "Hamlet *wants* to feel, I believe, and to be an actor on a stage outside his teeming head, but cannot as yet. In Wittenberg, where the mass are frivolous students, jesting in the foyer of real affairs, his lack—even madness of a sort, the madness of detachment—is not revealed; he should be a student forever. Here, amid earnest interests, he is challenged, and turns all to words and scorn. My hope is that love will lend him the right gravity. The fair Ophelia could not be bettered in her sweetness, her delicacy of apprehension. Your brother thought her too frail to serve his line, but she grows womanly, and Hamlet's interest grows apace."

"Very well," Claudius said, sated with wifely wisdom, and quite ready now to let this grand day go. "But your analysis brings with it another reason why he must not escape to Wittenberg. True attachment must build on increments, as you and I well remember."

She broke the silence his own had pointedly suggested. "My lord?"

"Yes, my queen? It is late. A king needs to greet the sun as an equal."

"Do you feel guilty?"

She felt his body stiffen, his breathing skip a breath. "Guilty concerning what?"

"Why, what else?—guilty concerning our, our coming together while . . . Hamlet was my husband."

Claudius snorted and hugged tighter his accumulating nugget of fatigue, making their featherbed emphatically heave. "The old Norse rule is, what you cannot hold is not yours. I took from him a property he didn't know he owned—territory he had never plowed. You were a virgin to unbridled love."

And, though she felt this as not entirely true, it was true enough to rest on, and they fell asleep in unison.

The Queen, some weeks after her wedding, summoned Ophelia to visit her in her closet, once King Roderick's new oriel room. The daughter of Polonius and his mourned Magrit had become in her eighteen years a luminous beauty, shy yet lithe, her skin pale and flawless, her waist willowy, her bosom high, her hips wide enough to declare her a vessel of nurture. She wore a blue mantle, a chaplet of gold braid, and a flowing gauzy gown almost indecent in its transparency. She carried herself with her chest lifted as if by a sharp, startled gasp, conveying an expectancy touchingly mingled with something wary and fragile. Gertrude looked upon her seeking her own young self, and saw that Ophelia's cheeks lacked a shade of rosiness and that her hair, brushed back from a glossy brow more ideally high than Gertrude's had ever been, was a bit thin and lacking in body; it did not spring up from her temples but lay docilely flat, held in place by the braided gold cord. Her face in profile was as cleanly stamped as a coin, yet frontally showed a certain vagueness, a tendency to direct her wide blue eyes a little off to the side. Her teeth, Gertrude noted not without envy, were perfect pearls, perfectly spaced. They were given an almost infantile roundness by her low, palely pink gums, and tilted very slightly inward, so her smile imparted a glimmering impression of coyness, with even something light-heartedly wanton about it.

Gertrude waved her toward the same bare-bottomed, three-legged chair that Polonius had occupied in their sessions of counsel. "My dear," she began. "How fares it with you? We women are so few at Elsinore, we owe each other the comfort of a tête-à-tête."

"Your Majesty flatters me. I feel still a child in this court, though attentions that lately come my way would call me out from my hiding corner." The girl had a lovely upper lip, turned both inward and outward like a plucked rose petal, slightly crumpled by its infusion of sweet plumpness, and it was fetching, Gertrude thought, the way it rested tentatively closed on the lower, leaving an open triangle through which her teeth dimly gleamed. Her nostrils were exquisitely narrow—Gertrude had always thought her own a little broad, her nose a trifle mannish and blunt.

"As women, we would not wish never to receive attentions, yet they can be alarming when they come."

"Indeed, exactly, Your Majesty." If Ophelia's character had a flaw, it was an excess of docility with yet, as in a child, an implicit defiance and secrecy. Her eyes, far from

Gertrude's gray-green, which could in passion darken like the Sund, reflected blank heavens in their pale blue.

"You need not call me 'Majesty,' nor can you quite call me 'Mother,' though I would like to serve you, in the absence of a mother, with kindness and advice. I, too, had a mother early dead, leaving me to make my way in a world of stone and men's clamor."

"Your Majesty has already shown me much kindness. As long as I can remember, you have been kind, and paid me notice, when few did."

"My kindness now takes on a closer quality. I believe the attentions you speak of have been coming from my son."

Ophelia's cloudless eyes widened but did not surrender that unsettling off-centeredness, as if focused on things invisible. What had King Hamlet irascibly said? *Her brain holds a crack.* "Some of them," she conceded, unsatisfactorily. "With Hamlet and Laertes both being home since your—since you and the new king—"

"Married, yes."

"They have been much together, and I am sometimes included."

"Dearest Ophelia, I fancy it is the other way around, that Hamlet, seeking *your* company, has found Laertes included perforce."

"In truth, they have a boisterous fondness for one another, and much in common. They have both accustomed themselves to wider horizons, and chafe at our backward and insular ways."

"I think, though you becomingly disclaim it, that you are being courted, and I am glad."

"Glad, madame?"

"Why not, my child? 'Tis natural for you, and overdue for him."

"My brother and my father both warn me, much more than once, against the dangers that beset virginity, and admonish me to know my price and guard my honor, which is theirs."

Gertrude smiled and leaned forward toward the maiden, as if to feel on her face the radiated warmth of youth. "But you—you find it hard to value so-called honor so highly? It seems to us a man's abstraction, for which they choose to preen and die, but which would debar us from the illuminations of love."

She was not sure, for a space of silence, if she had been understood, but then Ophelia let go her held-breath erectitude, in the comfortless triangular chair, and confessed limpidly, "Prince Hamlet does sometimes press me very hard. He makes me giddy with his words, and is antic enough to sound mad. The next instant, we laugh together, and I cease to be bewildered."

"He bewilders you?"

Ophelia blushed, lowering her gaze, and Gertrude was glad to see such proof of responsive blood. Had she been favored with a daughter, she would have loved her; she would have given her a guiding hand in the storms of feeling to which her sex was prone, and drawn her to her with no such struggle as a squirming son provides. Her mothering of Hamlet had been, Gertrude could not but feel, a failure, yet through this prospective wife she could touch him yet.

"At times," Ophelia explained, "his compliments seem a mockery; they claim too much of me. He quotes poetry, and even writes some."

"Claudius, too, resorts to verse," Gertrude dared disclose. "Men have a nature more divided than ours. They go from muck to mountaintop in their minds, and take no middle ground. To justify the demands of their bodies they must exalt the object of those demands into a goddess, an unlikely sublime, or else treat her as a piece of muck. My son is imaginative, and from boyhood has been enthralled by the theatrical. If he plays the lover to the hilt, it does not mean he plays falsely."

"So I have reasoned with myself. Hamlet has been my study since I was merely a set of eyes mounted on knobby stems. I was not yet ten when he turned twenty-one. He seemed to me, as to all observers, the epitome of a prince—exquisite in his dress, impeccable in form and command of language, an easy nobility in him to his fingertips. But now, in his pursuit of me, he will slip from good-natured flamboyance into near-disgust, as if a horror overtakes him in his wooing that turns his courteous effusions curt, and off he stalks without a God-be-wi'-ye. He is obscurely ornate and crudely frank in successive utterances, and makes no secret that he thinks my father lately a dotard, and ever a self-server."

"What does he say of his uncle, my husband?"

"He keeps his opinion from me, madame."

Gertrude doubted this—the rejoinder came too quickly—but pursued her main interest. How far had their wooing progressed? She scarcely recognized in

Ophelia's dazzled portrait her aloof and sullen son, who to her eye had always had a bit of his father's sallow puffiness. But it was proper to love's success that Ophelia be half blind. "You say he seems to mock you?"

"Amid many shows of tenderness and customary protestation."

Gertrude did not like the sound of "shows of tenderness." Had Ophelia already yielded that which could not be bartered back? Had she had the womanly wit to set her lover some trials, enhancing her worth in his eyes? Or in her heated innocence had she given him her body's ultimate pledge? There was something about this fey beauty in her gossamer dress that smelled not quite right, a touch polluted. She took Ophelia's hand from the girl's lap, where it had been flipping in undeclared disquiet. Gertrude was surprised at how moist the hand was, with a clammy damp.

"My child," she blurted, "enjoy your young years, they ebb soon enough. Follow your heart and head both, if you can. If my son and his lofty ties and his vagrant moods give you more confusion than pleasure, do not persist with him to please either your father or your queen."

"Oh, Papa is very definite that I must set a good value on myself; and yet I think the match would work to his advantage."

"Your father is full of years. He has had his advantages. Yours belong to you. Men," Gertrude said, abandoning all strategy in a gush of sisterly feeling, "men are beautiful enemies we are set down among. Without female compliance, the world would not get on, and yet they distrust our compliance, seeing in it the seeds of disorder, of random paternity. If we have been compliant with one man, they reason, we may be also with another. The wish to be agreeable we take in with our mothers' milk, alas." Gertrude felt her face warming but fought to keep a cool mien, knowing she was revealing more of herself than any woman but a mother should, and that only to her daughter.

Ophelia, however, was obsessed by her own condition and exclaimed, "Oh, I would want no one but Hamlet! I could never love another as I do him! If he deserted me, I would seek refuge in the convent, where life blows not so fierce."

"Deserted" seemed strong, if they were chaste. But, to be realistic, if Hamlet had indeed taken a bigger bite of this morsel than was proper, then he might be the more deeply hooked. Though the interview was giving her a qualm or two as to Ophelia's soundness, the Queen still believed that Hamlet should be married—marriage was the quickest way out of his sterile egotism, and a curtailment of the freedom of whim and motion that Claudius found menacing in his nephew. Marriage ties us to the established order. She released the shapely limp hand, with its delicate blue-green veins on the backs and wrists. "You do love Hamlet so?"

"With my life, Your Majesty, even when he is edgy with me, and prates of female fickleness."

Gertrude stiffened. "Is that what he prates of?"

"Yes, and our susceptibility to lust."

"As I say, our susceptibilities are the saving of them, and sometimes they even remember to be grateful."

"Hamlet can be infinitely tender, as if I might break."

"Oh? When is this?"

Ophelia's rose-petal upper lip lifted in thought. She lowered her lids on her eyes' bland sky and then opened them to say, "All of the time, when we are together, but for when he is thinking of some unnamed other, or of our sex in general. He hates the species, he says, but loves the individual."

"Too much German philosophy," Gertrude diagnosed. "It curdles every simplicity." Who could not love this guileless beauty, she asked herself, and be sane? "You have drawn closer to my son," she told Ophelia, "than I have been since I carried him below my heart."

"Trust me to cherish that closeness, and to do him no harm."

Gertrude heard a bit of complacency in this ready reply. "My fear does not run for him, my dear, but for you. Treat him as your instinct directs, but only to the point where you do not violate your instinct of self-protection. You and he have long lives to spend. It is good to love, good enough to stretch its stages out and hold its climax in long anticipation. For men, love is part of their ruthless quest for beauty; for us, it is more gently a matter of self-knowledge. It discovers us from within." Lest you think me a cynic on the topic of men, remember that I am myself a bride, and would not exchange my happiness for all the promises of Heaven."

"To be as gracious and wise as you, madame, is all I would wish for myself. If ever I can call you 'Mother,' I will do so with all my heart."

"And I will hear it with the same," said the Queen,

laughing at her own tears as the two women perfumed the closet with the stir of their embrace.

Polonius encountered the Queen in the pillared lobby, with its checkerboard tesselations echoed from the floor to the painted wall-border up against the ceiling. "My daughter was much comforted and cheered by her interview with you."

"She is an angel. Would that I had had a daughter, what ardent consultations we would have had! But it does not speak well of my son's attention if she stands in much need of comfort and cheer from others."

"She is young, far younger than he, and—"

"She is younger than he by little more than I was junior to the late king."

"And you found him callous and neglectful, as you confessed to me more often than I wished to hear."

"Was it so often? I strove to keep my dissatisfactions to myself. And surely they were not as severe as your summary adjectives suggest. He was busy with kingship, and I was perhaps conceited." She did wish the old man would cease alluding to her stale confidences and to their past collusions. Once in his debt, one remained there.

"Young and tender, my daughter is, as I was saying," said Polonius, "and he presumes upon his princeliness and melancholy to show his brusque, erratic humors too nakedly, jibing back and forth, so to speak, with too indelicate a hand on the tiller, for a maiden reared in the breathless hush of chastity. Laertes, yes, as befits a grow-

ing man, was not kept uncontaminate from the tavern
and its adjuncts, the house of sale and the gambling den,
my man Reynaldo keeping watch that his bruises did not
become wounds."

"It is the pity of a woman's education," Gertrude observed, "that it comes all at once, as she is plunged from
maiden virtue into married virtue. She is expected to go
in a night from total innocence to total knowing."

The old man, deaf to her points, was becoming over-
wrought. "Virtue is all of a woman's worth," he said.
"Virtue is what she takes to market. The Prince toys with
her, and I must tug her back. Their private intercourse
shall be curtailed, until his tenders of affection have a
more solid ring. She needs a remission from Hamlet's
haughty, caustic presence."

"Tug her back, and Ophelia may be yours to keep."

"Do not so slight her—a lessening of her attendance
will fan his fickle flame to the requisite steadiness. Ophelia is Magrit in all the freshness that repeated stillbirths
stole from her, and add to that a preternatural grace she
must have learned from the flowers of the wood. Have
you ever heard her sing?"

"At fêtes and winter entertainments, since she was a
child. A true voice, but slight, and cracked when she
pushes it too high."

"A sublime voice, and indeed there must be no pushing. My queen, have no fear for the match we both
desire. A little enforced withdrawal will but give the
Prince opportunity to reflect upon my daughter's worth."

Gertrude impatiently heard in all this the doddering

Lord Chamberlain's faith that human affairs could all be managed, manipulated with cogs and ratchets like millwheels and clocks, by a clever enough puppeteer. Her own sense was of tides, natural and supernatural, to which wisdom submits, seeking victory in surrender. The young lovers should be, she felt, left alone in desire's grip, to be lifted by it above the maze constructed by their elders. But in these opinions she knew Polonius and Claudius both would call her sentimental and irrational, yielding up all initiative to God, like a benighted peasant woman or infidel Muhammadan.

The old counsellor leaned closer still to her side, to confide, "In my view and that of others, he has suffered in never having been denied a whim or desire. He grew up without discipline, madame."

He meant her little Hamlet. Her long-dormant love for her son was being roused in self-defense. It was her privilege, not the old man's, to doubt her mothering. She responded, "He needed little, it seemed to us. His wits and tongue were quicker than his father's and mine, and anticipated every corrective thought of ours. When the King took him in hand, I lost touch, and could only admire from a respectful distance."

"The King was stern and commanding; he loomed to the boy like a god, in armor, on horseback. Yorick was the closest to a human father young Hamlet had, but was a drunken rascal, and could act as mentor in nothing but antics and folly."

"You sound as if you do not like your hoped-for son-in-law."

"He does not like me."

"Liking is not easy for him. He perceives too many sides of a person at once. But the King has generous hopes for him, and a budding fondness. He believes he can woo Hamlet to adhere to the court, thus making our government unassailable."

"Any government will be assailed, my lady, in this treacherous broken-up land, with its mulch of old feuds and slaughters. Yet if any man can keep order, it is Claudius. Already, I owe him my life."

"Your life?" How odd of old men still to value their lives, which the rest of the world can see to be stumpends, tatters useful not even as a pen wiper.

"I meant, Your Majesty, my position, my status, my life being so bound up with the Lord Chamberlain's accustomed dignities. But trust me, the King has done well by us both, in ways not necessarily apparent, when brave behavior was required."

She was puzzled. There seemed to be a secret. The lobby floor was tilting its alternating squares and threatening to open beneath her feet, while Polonius's prattle was trying to close the hole it had clumsily opened. "Ah," he rambled on, "we've come a long ways together, Your Highness. Remember the bright cold day I skied twelve leagues of fresh drifts to bear official witness that your bridal sheets were blood-stained? They were, I saw they were. You did not let royal honor down, before or since." He was thinking of his daughter, her virginity, preserved or surrendered.

"Bleeding," said Gertrude, "surely is among the lesser of a woman's accomplishments."

"Not in certain contexts, it is not. Blood rules the world, beneath all the courtesies. Or the lack of it, when a royal heir is hoped for. But enough; I'm rattling into immodesty." He adjusted his tall green sugarloaf hat, which sat more loosely on his head as his lank tallow-yellow hair thinned and the pumpkin-shell thickness of fat withered on his skull. *We begin small, wax great, and shrivel,* she thought. *The world discounts us before we discount ourselves.* "I merely meant to warn you, milady," Polonius rattled on, "that, when you hear I've asked Ophelia to play the miser regarding her private presence with the lord Hamlet, it's for the ultimate good of the conjugal hopes we share."

"She is your daughter to command," Gertrude said, hoping to conclude an uncomfortable interview. "I pray the ban will function as your calculations have persuaded you." All this thought given in the world to breeding, as if we are nothing but livestock, became tedious as well as unseemly. If the Prince's affection had mettle, he would kick through whatever fences were set up. She felt a kinship with her son, which she could not communicate, as his amorous will was tested. Poor boy, born like herself into the fine-grinding mill of Elsinore.

She roamed through the castle as if she were after a lifetime leaving it, mourning the little deserted solar where she had played with her three cloth dolls under the nodding care of Marlgar, and gazing toward the green-gray breadth of the Sund, flecked with ice and whitecaps, through a window to which she had so often lifted her stinging eyes from the embroidery frame or the shining vellum of a romance, a tale of Lancelot and Guinevere or of Tristan and Isolde, tales and *chansons* of adulterous but somehow sacred and undying loves.

When had she last worked on her embroidery? The piece on her frame, an altar cloth for the chapel, remained unchanged from the days before the King's death. Its background was executed in gold thread and underside couching; it showed, from a sketch in Gertrude's own hand, Mary of Magdala kneeling before the risen Christ. Wavy long hair carried out in parallel chain-stitches of alternating brown and black concealed her body but for a pink knee worked in satin-stitch, and her downcast pale profile with lowered lid, and one hand lifted as if to ward off the blessing gesture of the white-robed Lord. His outline had been pounced onto the linen from the design on pricked parchment and awaited its working in colored thread. Her mind in these months had been much with her lover and her husband, and she had trouble concentrating on yet a third man, though He was the ultimate Man. She had made a beginning on His feet, each toe outlined in slightly coarse stem stitch. When young she had taken pride in her split stitching, the needle piercing the thread itself, again and again, but years ago the point began to blur, and her vision needed more and more rest within the dull-colored distances toward Skåne. Now she wondered if she would ever again be settled in her soul enough to sit with her embroidery and untrembling hands while recorders played and her ladies-in-waiting gossipped in pattering snippets.

Gertrude roamed the perspectives of the castle, its arched arcades and spiral stairs, its slant-silled windows oddly placed where no one could look out of them, the pungent garderobes corbelled out above the moat, the chapel that seemed to her so much less impressively employed now than in the half-pagan days of King Roderick, the great hall that had held her two marriage feasts, its high beams hung with faded, rotting pennants captured in battle or given in tribute, its walls bearing quartered shields garish with the insignia of all Denmark's provinces, islands, and cathedral seats. Though Claudius was well into his second month of kingship, and asserted his authority in nightly banquet and daily audience, in uproarious celebration and well-weighed proclamation, Elsinore throughout all its stony maze, from its lowest dungeons to its highest paved battlement, still belonged in her sense of it to King Hamlet.

She thought of him, since her marriage to another, more and not less, as she would have expected, now that the crime of adultery and the fever of duplicity were alike receded, buried within her consecrated bridal status. Perhaps her son was right in his silent reproaches—his pointed absence from court events, his castigating costume of mourning's black. It had been too soon, though her suitor had marshalled invincible arguments; some matter had been left unfinished, unsounded. She kept expecting to see her former husband, as she often had done a mere season ago, in the turnings of a passageway, emerging from his low door with a puffy face from his nap in the orchard, or stamping into the courtyard in full armor from some combative exercise, fairly snorting like his lathered horse in the exhilaration of his own still-powerful body. And he had had less worldly exercises, too, for she would meet him returning down the long gallery to the chapel, where he had been seeking God's collusion in the rule of Denmark. Claudius, she noticed, rarely availed himself of such holy conference; he never made confession and when the bread and chalice came his way during Mass appeared to cringe, as if being constrained to sip poison, though unable to shirk, in the witness of those watching, the priest's pale hands nudging forward the cup and wafer, the wafer round like the white-glazed window above the altar.

King Hamlet in Gertrude's sense of him became almost palpable, quickening all of her senses save that of sight, her ears imagining a rustle, a footstep, a stifled groan, the nerves and fine hairs of her sixth sense tickled and brushed by some passing emanation, though the corridor was windless, and no newly snuffed candle or fresh-lit fire could account for the whiff of burning, of smoke, of char, of roasting. And upon this sense was visited an impression of pain; he seemed, this less than apparition but more than absence, to be calling her name, out of an agony—*Gerutha*, as she had been in the deeps of time. She felt dread; she was often unattended, for Herda was advanced in her pregnancy, and, at her years, much discommoded by it. Gertrude wanted no casual companion, no silly young lady-in-waiting, sent by some provincial court as spy, to intrude upon her restless patrol of Elsinore. So no one with her could confirm her imagination, when she halted nearly suffocated as if by a hand scorched yet icy clapped across her face.

What did dead Hamlet want of her? All-seeing from beyond the grave, he knew her sins now, every rapturous indecency and love-cry. Still, does not the liquid bath of

Heaven wash away the smut of this sphere? The blessed dead do not haunt the living; only the damned do, tied to the living fallen, and her late husband had been a model of virtue and a very pattern of kingship. *He wants me still to be his* was her intuition; the King loved her, had always loved her, and her infidelity, that while living he had in his royal preoccupations overlooked, now tormented him so that she could smell his burning flesh and almost hear his strangled voice.

Such thoughts were not natural; she sought to surmount them. Gertrude had always been able to turn toward the natural, trusting in what was obvious, what she could touch—the dyed threads of her embroidery, the feathery seed-bearing heads of the grasses—leaving to the Church the great craggy superstructure of which nature is but the face, the visible fraction, the forestage holding an evanescent drama. Confidently and universally the priests proclaim this sad and gaudy earth to be but the prelude to an everlasting afterlife, where Jesus and Moses and Noah and Adam will glower down like stone heads in a cathedral banked dazzlingly with supplicant candles. Now the natural had been tugged slightly awry; she felt, vaguely, pursued. In her bedchamber she tried to describe her sensation to Claudius, omitting her husband's name and the suspicion that Hamlet, dead Hamlet, was in the castle exerting a claim upon her.

Even Claudius felt the suspicion, for he had directed that they not, married, sleep in the same bed she and Hamlet had used, but in another solar of the royal apartments, in a Venetian bed with ivory inlay brought, in a long day's lumbering hay-wagon ride, from Lokisheim.

Out of habit she had more than once wandered, having risen in the night, toward her old chamber, where she met a locked door. She told Claudius, "I am happy, I am grateful, I am *pleased* and yet, dearest, something will not rest; it troubles me."

He said sensibly, "You have endured several shocks: suddenly a widow, and then soon a wife again." His tone was more judicious and, though affectionately, final than she had hoped for. "Your substance is not as elastic as it once was," he added. Was this a criticism? Did he already regret possession of her aging substance, coveted when she was far younger?

"Herda worries me, for one thing. She seems so bereft and sodden in her spirit, and the baby but a month from greeting the sun. I wonder it can grow. She thought Sandro loved her."

"He did, when he said he did. Then he became frightened of his ardor's consequences. She has no cause to fear for his child; Elsinore's economy can afford one more mouth. If she declines to love the infant, it will die."

"You sound so absolute."

"Without love, we die, or at best live stunted." He imposed, for emphasis, a firm kiss upon her mouth. He still maintained all the shows of love, defying her prejudice that it weakens a man's devotion when that devotion becomes lawful.

"Was that your experience in Jutland?" she asked him.

"It was bleak. We made do with half-portions."

"I, too, had a half-portion, after my mother died just as we could begin to converse. I was three."

He was suppressing, she saw, a male impatience with such exploration of idle feelings and a past beyond recall. "At three," he said, "I expect our bearing and courage are formed. Your mother loved you, and you bloomed. You bloom still, in my eyes." He heard his own words and looked at her steadily. Under his solemn dark stare she could not help smiling. He said, "I look at your smiling face and a hole is punched in the gloom of the world. Something better flows through from . . . from elsewhere. '*Tant fo clara,*' " he quoted, " ' *ma prima lutz d'eslir lieis don cre crel cors los huoills.* So clear it made it, my first flash of choosing her whose eyes my heart fears.' "

So romantic an avowal warranted an embrace, a kiss returned to his lips, lips once so potent in their molded shape and still able to stir her, to fluster her. Yet she could not stop seeking for what, elusively, was amiss in their circumstances, like a skipped stitch that might unravel the whole sleeve. "Did you help Sandro get away?"

"I did not," Claudius emphatically stated. "His defection took me by as much surprise as it did Herda. I had thought him loyal. It proves: only trust a Dane, and even then be wary."

"He must have needed some money, even walking. There is lodging, and food, and bribes at every border, for every little German princeling."

"Darling, why this harping? I would bring Sandro back, if he were within my realm. But he had passed out of it before it became mine."

Something in this—the strict timetable, the proud claim of acquisition—plucked at her disquiet. The approach of tears warmed her eyes, roughened her throat. "It's just that poor Herda, imitating us, now has this burden, and all we have is—happiness!"

"Yes, for me at least it is a great happiness. We did not ask Herda and Sandro to imitate us."

"We created a wanton atmosphere," she went on, tears and voice tumbling together in an erupted soreness, "and now she suffers with the evidence."

"I think, my dear, you are becoming—"

"You've shut me out somehow! There are things I don't know! Polonius was telling me you saved his life, but he won't tell me how. He implied I should be grateful to you, too, but for what? I mean, besides loving me and making me once more a queen?"

Claudius glowered in consideration; the darkening of his face made the scar-patch of white hair above his temple stand out brighter. "I fear our trusted friend and adviser may indeed be getting old. He rambles, he drops mysterious hints. My brother was right—the Lord Chamberlain is ripe for retirement."

She seized the opportunity to agree, not wanting the gulf between them to grow. "He does fuss at everything. He wants to forbid Ophelia from seeing Hamlet, hoping to regularize his courtship. He's afraid she's going to sleep with him and degrade herself in his eyes."

"Is that likely?"

The quick intensity of his interest snatched the words from her mouth for an instant. "I don't know," Gertrude weakly admitted. "She has a streak of strangeness. Hamlet—your brother—noticed it. He didn't think she was suitable for our son. He wanted a Russian princess."

She disliked evoking her late husband, but Claudius had mentioned him already— had brought him into the room.

"I want Hamlet near us," Claudius said.

He meant young Hamlet, she realized. "Oh, why?" she burst forth in honest, unnatural, unmotherly feeling. "He throws such a cloud."

"He would give our court a necessary unity. A trinity. The people don't want an anointed prince who is never here. In any case, I like him. I like young men who dislike Denmark. I think I understand him, and can help him."

"You do? How?" *These kings*, she thought. They never ceased to surprise her with their blithe attempts to be omnipotent.

"He blames himself, I believe, for his father's death," Claudius smoothly explained. "He feels he willed it, in desiring you."

"Me? He avoids me, and always has."

"That is the reason. You are too much woman for him, my dear, too warm for his comfort. He fled into coldness, idealizing his father and taking up German philosophy. He loves you, as I do, as any man with eyes and a heart must. He and I share something else: we were overshadowed by the same man, a man hollow but for his appetite for reputation. The Hammer was an oppressor; you felt it, too, or would not have betrayed him."

" 'Betrayed' seems harsh—augmented him, was how I felt it. Augmented him with you, at your incessant importunities. Dearest, you are less than just to your brother. You become unreal on the subject. You have— did have—much in common, all the more so, now that you are king."

"My brother reminded me, always, unpleasantly of Jutland—that terrible *lowness* of the view, the bogs and mists and heath, the sheep and the rocks thinking the same deadly thought day after day, that is, how satisfied they were to be what they were, at the exact windblown center of the universe. But that is past. To the issue at hand: I want you to love Hamlet. Hamlet your son."

"I do. Do I not?"

"In a franker mood you have professed not. Now make a fresh start. Greet him, engage him. Don't expect an immature girl to do all your work of restoration. Cease to be afraid of him, Gertrude."

"I *am* afraid of him, yes!"

This confession, with all her smoldering terror suddenly ablaze in it, did throw Claudius off stride, as he swung back and forth undressing, pontificating as King Hamlet used to do. "What is to fear? He brings us only a troubled heart, begging to be healed. He knows his future is here."

"I am afraid of the war he brings within himself. You and I have made a peace, on terms allowed by a tragic mishap, and Denmark has set you peaceably on the throne. My son in his nighted color and spicy-red beard may unsettle all these fine arrangements."

"How can the boy? He has nothing but his expectations. The power is ours, to share. I have no son, but hope to play the father to yours."

She surrendered, as was her wont. "Your hope is generous and loving, my lord; it shames me. And shames Hamlet as well, if he could know it. I will be glad to follow your lead and attempt to act a mother's part."

Already, during her talk of Hamlet with poor smitten Ophelia, she had felt a renewal of fondness, as if in plotting his marriage she were carrying him again within her—*below my heart*, she had said. Her resentment of the bond he had adamantly formed with his father was receding, and with it doubt of her maternal effectiveness. Through her tender, piteous intimacy with Ophelia she had seen that the generations need not be inimical, the younger impatient for the older's ruin. And still—"Still, my dear husband, why do I have this dread?"

Claudius laughed, showing his wolfish teeth in his soft beard. "You have acquired, my sweet Gertrude, what the rest of us are born with or soon acquire, an unease of the soul. You have ever been too much at home in the world. This unease, this guilt for our first father and mother's original sin, is what calls us to God, out of our unholy pride. It is the sign He has placed within us of His cosmic rule, lest we think we are the very top of the universal hierarchy." He laughed again. "How I do love you—that cautious glance as you puzzle at how much of what I say I say to tease you. I do tease, but with a feather of truth. All my life I have been gnawed, feeling but half a man, or a real man's shadow. No more: you flesh me out. 'I am in her service,' the poet says, *'del pe tro c'al coma*—from my foot to my hair.' Come, wife, let me see you undress. In Byzantium," he went on, with a docent's wide gesture, "in wastelands beyond the reach of iconoclastic potentates and censorious monks, ruins a thousand years old present to the sun roofless pillars and broken statues of naked women—goddesses, perhaps, from before Eve's disobedience. You are their sister. The glory of you lavishes balm on my uneasy spirit; the Creation that has you in it, wife, must hold salvation for the vilest sinner. You are my virtue and my plague, of which I defy all cure."

"You speak out of all proportion, my lord," she objected, yet continued to disrobe. The bedchamber's air clothed her in a film of cold that stiffened her nipples and made the pale hair of her forearms rise up.

His eyes took her in and his voice and gestures became extravagant. "Behold, you shiver, and your throat and shoulders blush to the verge of your breasts, so wildly Heaven-storming sounds my praise! Not so. It is honest. You render me honest. You are conjunctive to my soul, as the heretic troubadours expressed it. We have outgrown beauty, the young of the world might judge, but our senses swear otherwise. Here, Gertrude, I will be the fur rug spread ahead of your naked feet. I will warm the icy bed with my burning old bones!"

And she did glimpse something of beauty in his fattened white shanks and hair-darkened buttocks and bobbing roused member as he scuttled underneath the covers, his teeth in their beard chattering while his feet sought the swaddled hot bricks servants had placed between the sheets. She had feared, of herself and Claudius, that their passion might not survive the transition from adultery's fearful wilderness to the security of proclaimed marriage; but it had. In that way they had proven both sturdy, and worthy of the trouble and labor of mating. Being with Claudius in bed was meeting herself come from afar, a forthright and unforced reunion.

.   .   .

The King was ebullient. Last night had been bitter cold, the stars a merciless icy spatter, but this morning a sunny wind whipped the froth in plumes from the whitecaps in the Sund, and a bustle of action sounded throughout Elsinore. An official audience was scheduled for this morning, St. Stephen's Day, and whatever of ineradicable unease clung to his soul, and whatever black remorse remained of the vial of poison he had poured into his sleeping brother's ear (the waxy hole, at the center of the universe, had seemed to drink thirstily, to suck the very zenith from the sky), these ghosts were banished by the sunlight that flooded the great hall; the flames in the two great arched fireplaces paled in the solar beams admitted by the high, unshuttered clerestory windows. The sky outside showed an unsullied blue, clearer than the conscience of a saint. *All comes clean*, Claudius thought, *under Heaven's wheel.*

Two months had passed since his brother's death, and a month since he had with bold haste taken to wife King Hamlet's widow. His opening remarks to the assembled court would address both these untoward contingencies, and by describing them, frankly yet tactfully, relegate them to history, as building blocks of the foundation upon which his reign rested. He would remind his councillors that he acted with their approval; he would acknowledge that, in choosing to wed so soon, his discretion had warred with nature, but that, after all, he, Claudius, was alive, and had to think of himself as well as, with wisest sorrow, his dead dear brother. Life was framed by such paired contraries.

Phrased with a grave and artful balance, making music

of dirge in marriage and of contrasting delight and dole, this exposition would serve as a sop to Hamlet, who was putting on an ostentatious show of his mourning costume and, with many overheard sighs and asides in dubious taste, was letting it be known that he resented his mother's swift capitulation to his uncle's suit. Claudius could coldly see that he and his nephew, now stepson as well, might come to a hard enmity, but for now all the effort was to be of reconciliation, as one makes up to a sulking child, ignoring immaturity's ill-formed insults and spreading wide the arms of paternal forbearance.

He would remind, too, his auditors that Gertrude was no accidental queen but herself closely tied by blood to Denmark's throne, indeed an "imperial jointress"—a pregnant phrase whose resonance would not be lost on any who harbored thoughts that his claim to the throne was weak and his election in any way irregular in its efficient haste. Polonius, too, he must professedly knit close to his royal authority, as close as the heart to the head, or the hand to the mouth, this Lord Chamberlain for the king's two revered predecessors.

The devious old courtier, with his uneven and garrulous wits, should be reassured in public that his service was still valued and, it could be implied, along with his service his co-conspiratorial silence. Were Polonius ever to be retired, it unpleasantly crossed Claudius's mind, it must be to the silence of the grave, rather than to any intermediate station, such as the cozy dwelling by Gurre Sø, wherefrom he might suffer temptation to be restored, with sale of his secrets, to power. Murder and usurpation, alas, are acids so potent they ever threaten to dissolve the barrel in which they have been sealed.

But now the court, the state, and the nation, in widening rings of attention, must be reassured. Though his grip on the sceptre felt secure, a shakiness pervaded the public mind. The preparations for a defensive war that that overweening pup young Fortinbras, seeking to reëmbody his father's militant spirit, had forced upon Denmark filled even the Sabbath air with the sounds of halberts being forged and ships being pounded and pegged together. Affairs trembled on the edge of fantasy; it was rumored that battlement sentries on the midnight watch had been seeing an apparition in full armor. This morning, in clear and ringing syllables, the King will allay the general unease with a diplomatic mission: Cornelius and Voltemand are to be dispatched with documents whose every article bears the impress of resolute ponderation, to Norway, younger son of the slain Koll and an infirm relic of a heroic age, bedridden and impotent yet with still the regal power to forbid. Claudius's detailed missive will inform him that his nephew on his own initiative, out of levies and resources that are Norway's and not his own, intends a rash sortie. Claudius knows first-hand of this modern age's reluctance to risk rebellion, among nobles or populace, in the wake of bloody adventurism for fleeting gains; the Crusades and their long-range failure have taken the heroism out of battle. Old Norway, the elder Fortinbras's effete and gouty younger brother, will suppress his hot-blooded kinsman, and Denmark will fatten in the peace its shrewd and prudent monarch has arranged.

In anticipation of these diplomatic triumphs—of feeling the very ribs of his chest reverberate in projecting his voice to the far corners of the hall—he squeezed the Queen's resilient arm, under the concealment of their dragging robes, as they processed, bestowing smiles and nods, through the colorful ranks of Elsinore's attendant population. Hamlet was there, looking ill-slept and sour, his red beard complemented by a velvet tricorne, which he removed with an ironical flourish as Gertrude and Claudius passed. The King wondered about the sleeplessness that set such a pallor on his face—up till the russet dawn with Ophelia, sullying his flesh? She was not here, still abed: a novice slut. Young Laertes, appearing in contrast altogether fit and rested, with a close, pointed Parisian cut to his beard and a smartly snug doublet that stopped short of his codpiece, stood erect at the side of his shrunken father. The two had some innocuous petition, the King had been forewarned. Though Polonius had doffed his sugarloaf hat and bowed low, exposing his bald pate and straggly sorcerer's locks, Claudius saw that the old man's gleaming eyes darted everywhere. He gave the King a wink, could this be? Or was it just a trick of the moment's dust and sunbeams? The impression at any rate was unpleasant, and Claudius, cautiously nodding in response, made a mental note that his Lord Chamberlain's retirement must be arranged.

How wonderful it was, the way that a king's robes bring in their ermine-trimmed heaviness a spiritual investment lending each minor action a major implica-

tion—a single fingertip moving through an arc of conse-
quence with the power of a sword. To be thus, an entire
nation concentric to his pumping heart, and all the rev-
erence and hopes of a people arrowing toward him from
the remote domains of Thy and Fyn, Møn and Skåne,
was to be a man at last, his potential actual, his every
thought and action magnified with eternal significance.
He felt a black pang, there at the focus of all eyes including those great invisible ones peering from Heaven,
through the clerestory windows. His offense was rank,
with the primal curse upon it. Yet whereto served mercy
but to confront the visage of offense? Time abounded
in which to make his accounts right, through penitence
and prayer. After his feats, this too seemed feasible; the
Church made its intercessions as available as daily bread,
and scarcely more expensive.

As he and the Queen, in the unison of a stately dance,
took the three steps up to the throne dais, the thought
of bread brought back their round room in the borrowed
lodge, their picnic repasts often lost in the feast of their
lust, and that day of rain, a rain pounding the fresh fo-
liage into a green mist seen through the narrow pointed
window, with a pellmell thrumming on the slates, when
she, having resolved to make an end of him, instead
slipped off her new silk robe and showed herself to him
as she would be on the Day of Resurrection emerging
naked from the tomb, forgiveness being on that day dis-
pensed as freely as the loaves and fishes.

Ebulliently he felt her silent body, possessed, alive
beside his. He glanced her way and, sensing his glance,
uncertain whether to smile here at the height of cere-

mony, Gertrude did quickly smile. Whenever he saw her afresh—the calm gray-green eyes, the ingratiating small space between her front teeth, the rosy complexion of a child heated by hope and play, the coppery hair unruly even beneath the weight of her golden crown—he realized what was, simply, real, all else being an idle show of theatrical seeming.

The royal couple took their two thrones, whose coat of gilt had not prevented rot from nibbling at the ancient sticks of linden and ash, including it was said bits of the True Cross and of the primal tree Yggdrasil. Claudius spoke his lines so all could hear. The speech went well, he thought. The regrets and compliments were distributed with a calm grace, the general collusion in his actions tersely made clear, and the situation with Fortinbras and the King's response ringingly outlined. Laertes, having done his duty in attending the King's coronation, asked for leave to go back to Paris, and this of course was granted, with compliments to Polonius that only the self-important old courtier would not recognize to be distancingly excessive.

Then, when Hamlet rebuffed with some muttered puns the King's fatherly inquiry after his health, Gertrude surprised Claudius by speaking up at his side, entreating her son to stop looking for his father in the dust. "All that lives must die," she gently told him, "passing through nature to eternity." Not the least of the King's reasons for loving her was that female realism which levelly saw through the agitations and hallucinations of men.

And when the boy—boy! thirty years old!—wordily implied, with the whole court listening, that only he was truly grieving King Hamlet, Claudius took it upon himself to continue her instruction in the obvious: men die, each father in turn has lost a father, it is unmanly and impious to persist in unavailing woe. "Think of us as of a father," he commanded, reminding him, "You are the most immediate to our throne." He elaborated on this theme of his love, and as he spoke, one iambic cadence smoothly succeeding another, Claudius was distracted by a clatter of birds—starlings, he guessed, shriller-voiced than rooks—at the blue clerestory windows above. The birds, scenting spring here at the height of winter, were stirred up and flocking to the sun-warmed roof of crumbling slates.

Some persons in attendance glanced up, the drama before them having perhaps stretched long. The day was revolving overhead, dropping rhomboids of sun upon the multi-colored finery and the hall's broad oak planks, worn and scarred. In olden days bored knights would clatter their horses up the stone stair and joust beneath the beams, where captured pennants faded and frayed.

Claudius finished with Hamlet by bluntly stating— where others had been pussyfooting for years—that he did *not* want Hamlet to return to Wittenberg: "It is most ret-rograde to our desire." He relished the imperious ring of this, but softened it by beseeching his stiff nephew to bend, to stay here, in Elsinore, "here in the cheer and comfort of our eye, our chiefest courtier, cousin, and our son."

Gertrude played her part, adding, "Let not thy mother lose her prayers, Hamlet: I pray thee, stay with us; go not to Wittenberg."

Trapped by their twin professions of love, the Prince

from beneath his clouded brow studied the two glowing middle-aged faces hung like lanterns before him—
hateful luminaries fat with satisfaction and health and
continued appetite. He tersely conceded, to shunt away
the glare of their conjoined pleas, "I shall in all my best
obey you."

"Why," Claudius exclaimed, startled by the abrupt
concession, " 'tis a loving and a fair reply." They had
him. He was theirs. The King's imagination swayed forward to the sessions of guidance and lively parry he
would enjoy with his surrogate son, his only match for
cleverness in the castle, and to the credit such a family
relation would win him in the heart of the boy's newly
fond mother.

The era of Claudius had dawned; it would shine in
Denmark's annals. He might, with moderation of his
carousals, last another decade on the throne. Hamlet
would be the perfect age of forty when the crown descended. He and Ophelia would have the royal heirs
lined up like ducklings. Gertrude would gently fade, his
saintly gray widow, into the people's remembrance. In his
jubilation at these presages the King, standing to make
his exit, announced boomingly that this gentle and unforced accord of Hamlet sat so smiling to his heart that,
at every health he would drink today, the great cannons
would tell the clouds. And his queen stood up beside
him, all beaming in her rosy goodness, her face alight
with pride at his performance. He took her yielding hand
in his, his hard sceptre in the other. He had gotten away
with it. All would be well.

Afterword

THE ACTION of Shakespeare's play is, of course, to follow. To Kenneth Branagh's four-hour film of *Hamlet* in 1996 the author owes a revivified image of the play and of certain off-stage characters such as Yorick and King Hamlet. A hint of Claudius's foreign soldiering can be found in IV.vii.83–84. His seductive gifts are mentioned by the Ghost at I.v.43–45. Salvador de Madariaga's *On Hamlet* (1948, rev. 1964) lists some of the play's many careless inconsistencies—the apparent invisibility of Horatio prior to Hamlet's greeting of him at I.ii.160, though he has been at Elsinore for two months, and the strangeness of a climate that goes in four months from a nap in the orchard to "bitter cold" on the battlements and thence to Ophelia's gathering of May and June flowers—and emphasizes Hamlet's impenetrable self-centeredness, drawing a parallel between the Prince's contempt for his auditors and the playwright's for his audience. William Kerrigan's *Hamlet's Perfection* (1994), a wholly positive and enthusiastic exposition of the play, contains this haunting summary of G. Wilson Knight's reading in *The Wheel of Fire: Interpretations of Shakespearean Tragedy* (1930; rev. 1949):

Putting aside the murder being covered up, Claudius seems a capable king, Gertrude a noble queen, Ophelia a treasure of sweetness, Polonius a tedious but not evil counsellor, Laertes a generic young man. Hamlet pulls them all into death.

A Note About the Author

John Updike was born in 1932, in Shillington, Pennsylvania. He graduated from Harvard College in 1954, and spent a year in Oxford, England, at the Ruskin School of Drawing and Fine Art. From 1955 to 1957 he was a member of the staff of *The New Yorker*, and since 1957 has lived in Massachusetts. He is the father of four children and the author of fifty previous books, including collections of short stories, poems, and criticism. His novels have won the Pulitzer Prize, the National Book Award, the American Book Award, the National Book Critics Circle Award, and the Howells Medal.

A Note on the Type

The text of this book was set in a digitized version of Janson, a typeface long thought to have been made by the Dutchman Anton Janson, who was a practicing type founder in Leipzig during the years 1668–1687. However, it has been conclusively demonstrated that these types are actually the work of Nicholas Kis (1650–1702), a Hungarian, who most probably learned his trade from the master Dutch type founder Dirk Voskens. The type is an excellent example of the influential and sturdy Dutch types that prevailed in England up to the time William Caslon developed his own incomparable designs from them.

Composed by Creative Graphics,
Allentown, Pennsylvania
Printed and bound by R. R. Donnelley,
Harrisonburg, Virginia